LION OF LANGUEDOC

Accused of witchcraft and hunted by Louis XIV's fanatical Inquisitor, Marietta Riccardi is only rescued from being burned alive by the intervention of Léon de Villeneuve – the Lion of Languedoc. Small wonder that she falls in love with him! Yet Léon is on his way to marry his childhood sweetheart, Elise, and to him Marietta is nothing but a tiresome peasant girl ... beautiful and seductive perhaps, but an unwelcome distraction from his forthcoming wedding. Marietta knows that she should leave France – escape hcr persecutors and her hopeless love – yet she cannot tear herself away from Languedoc, or from Léon...

LION OF LANGUEDOC

Lion Of Languedoc

by

Margaret Pemberton

Dales Large Print Books
Long Preston, North Yorkshire,
BD23 4ND, England.

British Library Cataloguing in Publication Data.

Pemberton, Margaret
    Lion of Languedoc.

    A catalogue record of this book is
    available from the British Library

    ISBN   1-84262-099-1 pbk

First published in Great Britain 1981 by Mills & Boon Limited

Copyright © Margaret Pemberton 1981

Cover illustration © Len Thurston by arrangement with
P.W.A. International Ltd.

The moral right of the author has been asserted

Published in Large Print 2001 by arrangement with
Margaret Pemberton, care of Caroline Sheldon

Dales Large Print is an imprint of Library Magna Books Ltd.

Printed and bound in Great Britain by
T.J. (International) Ltd., Cornwall, PL28 8RW

For Wendy Forbes
with many thanks

Chapter One

'The witch! The witch!' The demented cries rang in Marietta Riccardi's ears as she fled sobbing and stumbling down the dark hillside towards the thick cover of the forest. Behind her, livid tongues of flame scorched the night sky and there was nowhere to run to. Nowhere to hide.

'Blessed Jesu,' she gasped, thorns and briars tearing at her outstretched hands as she ran blindly between the first of the trees. *'Help me! Oh merciful heaven! Help me!'*

Léon de Villeneuve looked at the innkeeper with distaste. 'I've no desire for a burning. Give me another tankard of ale and I'll be on my way.'

The innkeeper shrugged. The stranger had the appearance of a chevalier. His doublet and breeches were of fine material and the short velvet cloak hanging jauntily from one shoulder exposed a fine sword. His bucket-top boots were of soft yellow leather trimmed with muddied lace and there was a further profusion of lace at his neck and cuffs. None of it detracted from his air of martial swagger. He was clearly not a man to trifle with, and the innkeeper had no intention of doing so. He had gold in his purse and the more he spent in his inn the better. There were no other customers. Every last man was on Valais Hill to see the burning of old Mother Riccardi. There was the granddaughter too. He smiled gloatingly. It would be good to hear *that* little hussy begging for mercy.

'What did the old hag do?' the stranger asked mockingly, cutting in on his thoughts. 'Blight the crops or turn a cow dry?'

'She cursed the Duvals' baby so that it sickened and died, *and* she had a familiar *and* she flew by night,' he added as his audience remained unimpressed.

Léon laughed. 'Did her familiar have cloven hooves and a horn?'

'You may jest,' he said defiantly. 'Pierre Vallin saw Beelzebub himself sitting on the thatch of her cottage. Black as night he was, and with a tail a yard long.'

'She confessed, did she?' Léon asked, wondering if his horse would be sufficiently rested for him to continue his journey.

'Screamed it from the rooftops,' the innkeeper said with satisfaction. 'Leastways she would have done but old Beelzebub looks after his own. She was dead before the inquisitor had finished with her.'

'How inconvenient.'

'It was hardly worth the burning of her,'

10

the innkeeper agreed disappointedly. 'I shan't miss the next, though. I'd give a good few francs to see what *that* one looks like without her shift on!'

Léon pushed his empty tankard away from him in disgust. The innkeeper, loth to lose his audience, no matter how disinterested, said, 'They'll be bringing her down for trial within the hour – have another ale. There'll be more entertainment in Evray tonight than you'll get for thirty leagues around!'

'My pleasure lies in different directions,' Léon said drily, striding towards the door and the inn yard.

'Arrogant young bull,' the innkeeper said beneath his breath. 'He'll have no trouble keeping his bed warm with his strong body and black curls.'

Mindful of the gaunt shrew of a wife who was *his* only solace, he reached bad-temperedly for his mug of ale. There had been no chance for *him* to join in the fun tonight. His wife had seen to that. 'There may be a passing traveller,' she had said, tight-lipped and hard-eyed. 'If there is we need his custom. No sense turning away *sols* for the sake of the Riccardis.' So, while the rest of his companions whooped it up on Valais Hill, he remained at his post. That his wife had been proved right did nothing to sweeten his temper.

Defiantly he thrust his mug to one side.

They would have to look for the witches' mark on Marietta Riccardi and he wasn't going to miss that pleasure for anyone. On the inside of the thigh was the usual place. His throat tightened at the thought. The trial would be held at the magistrate's house and if he wanted a front seat he would have to hurry.

Léon was already in the saddle when there came the sound of clattering hooves and raised voices. A man little older than Léon, with a cloak of velvet and a gleam of steel at his side, galloped into the yard, his horse wheeling angrily as he shouted, 'The witch has escaped! We need fresh horses! Men!'

In the moonlight Léon saw the fevered eyes, the cruel tightening of sensuous lips. It seemed it wasn't only the rabble of Evray who were eager for a burning; the diamond on the gloved hand was the size of a nut. He felt a wave of revulsion. He had killed many men in his time fighting for Louis, but he had never killed a woman. Or indulged in the soldiers' sport of rape. Women fell easily enough without being taken in front of dying husbands and crying children.

The innkeeper rushed to his stables, frantically summoning help in saddling every available horse he had. As he did so a dark-robed figure rode into the mêlée, surrounded by a seething mass of hysterical villagers.

'Get more men!' he commanded icily. 'Get torches! By God and all the holy angels, I'll have that strumpet before dawn!'

Léon laughed at the bitter frustration on the finely drawn features. 'It looks as if you've been cheated of your night's entertainment,' he shouted across the sea of frenzied faces to the innkeeper. 'Perhaps the Devil does look after his own!' and he dug in his spurs, forcing the Inquisitor's horse to one side as he galloped out of the yard and towards the road leading south.

The night sky was black, the moon masked by heavy cloud. Behind him he could hear the cries of the witch-hunters like a pack of baying wolves, the surrounding fields already alive with flickering torches as every man, woman and child joined in the hunt.

He didn't fancy the old hag's chances. The most she could hope for was to die of fear or exhaustion before they captured her. The snake-like eyes of the Inquisitor had chilled even his hardened bones. The fire on top of the hill still glowed and he averted his gaze. He was as good a Catholic as the next man, but these rabid inquisitions turned his stomach. They were a fever that his village of Chatonnay had never suffered from and the sooner he was back there, the better.

For six years he had been in the service of his King. His gallantry on the battlefield had soon brought him to Louis' notice and to court, and it hadn't been long before it was widely rumoured that de Villeneuve's prowess in the field of war was only equalled by his prowess in the art of love. Many husbands had cause to wish the dark-eyed, gipsy-faced Léon de Villeneuve back fighting the King's enemies and at the wrong end of a fatal sword-thrust. They were unlucky. Instead he became a regular member of the King's entourage, and the only wound he received at war was a rapier thrust on his hard lean body that only served to make him even more dashing in the eyes of the ladies who were fortunate enough to find their way into his bed.

There had been more than one masculine sigh of relief when Léon de Villeneuve had announced his intentions of returning to his home at Chatonnay. Even the ravishing Francine Beauvoir had been unable to tempt him to stay. Married to one of Louis' ministers, she had more airs and graces than Queen Marie-Theresa herself, but to Léon she was as much a whore as the willing women in the brothels of Spain. He grinned to himself in the darkness. There would be no more whoring when he had married Elise.

Old anger swept over him afresh. She had been seventeen when he had left Chatonnay, her hair the colour of summer corn, violet-blue eyes set in the innocent face of an angel, and old Caylus had heartlessly married her to a man old enough to be her grandfather. All Léon's pleadings had been in vain. The Villeneuves might own half the land around Chatonnay, but it was poor land and the family were impoverished. Léon was not a suitable husband for the daughter of a man who was cousin to a Duc.

Léon's mouth tightened at the thought of what Elise must have suffered in her marriage to the elderly, debauched mayor of Lancerre. Now she was a widow and he had ridden night and day since hearing the news, intent only on reaching her side in the fastest time possible.

The road wound deeper into the trees, so rutted and pitted that he had to slow his horse to a cautious walk. He ducked to avoid a low-hanging branch, cursing as the rough bark caught at his hair. Then he froze, reining in his horse. There was another sound in the thick blackness, the harsh gasping of an animal in pain. It came again, a pitiful moan quickly stifled.

'God's grace,' he whispered beneath his breath. 'The witch...'

There was the cracking of twigs and the rustle of leaves and then silence. His horse snorted impatiently, stamping the ground. He stroked its neck soothingly, waiting for another movement. None came. In the stillness the wind carried the faint cries of the

15

witch-hunters and the ground throbbed with the distant galloping of hooves. Another five minutes and the forest would be alive with men and torches, and the terrified old woman hiding only yards away from him would be at their mercy. He swung lightly from his saddle and immediately there was a muffled sob.

'Don't run,' he called, stepping from the track into the thick undergrowth, his eyes straining to see in the darkness.

Marietta pushed herself away from the tree-trunk, her heart feeling as if it would burst within her as she plunged wildly away from him. There was no escape now. She had only minutes left. The horse whinnied and Marietta clutched at a last frail straw of hope. She veered sharply, running headlong back towards the track, heedless of the leaves that whipped across her face and the tangle of roots that threatened to trip her at every step. His horse! If she could only reach his horse!

'Don't run!' Léon shouted exasperatedly. 'Mother of God, I'm trying to *help* you!'

She could see the dark outline of the waiting animal, see the bridle gleaming in the darkness, feel its warm breath on her cheek. Desperately her hand reached up, and at the same moment her shoulders were seized viciously and she was dragged to the ground.

'No you don't, you old beldame!' Léon gasped, gripping her wrists and pulling her arms behind her back as she lay writhing face down on the leaves. He placed his knee hard into the centre of her back. No wonder the villagers thought her a witch! Any hag who could run so far and so fast was worthy of the name.

The sound of hoofbeats was nearer now, the flicker of torchlight like fireflies in the distance. Momentarily distracted, his hold weakened. Marietta twisted on to her back, her freed hands clawing at his eyes. He rolled his full weight on top of her, grasping her wrists so hard that she cried out in pain, dragging them high above her head. Pinioned and unable to move, Marietta saw thick black hair tumbling over straight brows and dark eyes. He stared at her incredulously.

'Hell's light...' he whispered, feeling the firm breasts beneath his chest and the long legs trapped between his own. 'A wench...'

There were sudden voices and the clatter of hooves and when Léon leapt to his feet, scooping her up in his arms, Marietta did not protest. Instinct told her that her prayers had been answered. He swung into the saddle, dragging her up behind him, and with her arms tight around his waist set off at full gallop down the tortuous track.

Marietta clung on, the pounding of blood

in her ears merging with that of the following horsemen so that it seemed to her they could be only inches behind. The track swung to the left, growing narrower and shelving steeply, and still the horse kept its pace. Léon glanced behind him. The flickering torches had disappeared, all that could be heard was the relentless pounding of hoofbeats.

He listened hard, every nerve straining. There were two horses, perhaps three, certainly no more. He spurred his own beast to fresh efforts. That meant that the searchers were concentrating on the area of forest she could have reached by foot – after all, they had no reason to think he would aid a fleeing witch. He remembered his conversation with the innkeeper and felt less sure. He had made his opinion of the Evray witch-hunters only too clear, and if the innkeeper had the wit to transfer his knowledge to the gimlet-eyed Inquisitor, then more horsemen would be following and there would be little chance of either of them leaving the forest alive.

There was a cry of fright from behind him. *'They're coming!* You won't let them take me? Won't let them burn me?'

'They'll not have that pleasure,' Léon said grimly, glancing behind him and seeing two horsemen, their cloaks billowing in the wind as their horses swept round the last of the bends and came on at a gallop, manes flying, glistening necks outstretched.

'Blessed Jesu!' she whispered, her arms tightening around his waist. 'Faster! *Faster!*'

Léon cursed. There was no way he could outride them. His horse had already ridden many miles that day and had only had a short rest: theirs were fresh. The track sloped down suddenly and there was the glitter of running water. Léon crouched low in the saddle, steadying the animal's head, checking the wild gallop as the horse gathered itself at the stream's edge and leaped the wide swirl of water. He gained a few minutes' time as the horses behind him slithered to a rasping halt at the stream's bank, veering and snorting in dismay. Angrily their riders wheeled them round, heading for the stream again and taking it with a heave of quarters and a scramble of hooves.

Léon felt his horse lose pace and the thudding behind grew and swelled, bursting around them as a reedy voice shouted: 'There she is! Hold fast, sir!'

Léon smiled grimly to himself. The voice wasn't that of a fighting man. A horse gleaming with sweat began to draw abreast and a gloved hand grabbed wildly at Marietta, trying to drag her to the ground.

She screamed, her arms feeling as if they would leave their sockets as she clung on with every ounce of strength she had. The animals were level now and the gloved hand, failing to unseat her, snatched at Léon's reins. Léon struck down with such force that he nearly severed the offending hand from its owner's arm.

There was a cry of pain and then the second rider tried to head Léon off from the other side. Out of the corner of his eyes Léon saw a powerfully built man lean across, tearing Marietta from her hold. As Léon felt the clutching hands weaken he had no choice but to rein in, bringing his horse to a slithering halt.

'The wench is a witch!' the owner of the gloved hand shouted to him, as his burly companion succeeded in dragging a shrieking Marietta across his own horse. The nervous edge to his voice indicated that he would be only too pleased if Léon would profess his innocence of this knowledge and continue on his way without more ado. Léon wheeled around in time to see Marietta's captor wind a calloused hand into her mane of curls, half yanking them from the roots, the other reaching high under the torn gown.

With difficulty Léon restrained himself, facing his lesser adversary first.

'The Devil she is!' he said in feigned surprise, riding up to him.

The thin shoulders visibly relaxed. 'Aye, so

we'll trouble you no more, sir.'

Léon grinned at him in agreement and with the full force of his knotted fist punched him hard in the belly. There was a look of shocked surprise as the man rasped for breath, toppling sideways, his feet caught in the stirrups.

With an oath the other lunged at him from the rear, a muscled arm encircling his throat, pulling tight against his windpipe. Half choking, Léon hit backwards with his elbow, the blow glancing off a stomach that seemed made of iron. Struggling vainly for the hilt of his sword, he could feel his eyes bulging, his tongue protruding between his teeth, and then Marietta hurtled from the horse and sank her teeth deep into the assailant's thigh.

With a bellow of pain the grip around his throat eased and Léon's hands shot up and back, circling the bull-like neck and dragging the man from his stirrups and over his head with a massive heave. As he thudded to the ground Léon leapt towards him, his hand reaching for his sword.

He was seconds too late. His opponent rolled swiftly over, scrambling to his feet, charging into Léon like a crazed bull, head low and fists swinging, before Léon had unsheathed his sword.

Marietta saw a clenched fist slam hard into Léon's chest and heard his grunt of pain as he hit back. Then they were locked together, lurching and swaying, the horses whinnying excitedly, one bridle held by a gloved hand as its owner backed away nervously from the fight. She saw Léon's hand grope urgently for his sword, saw the other's foot kick hard, unbalancing him so that they rolled and struggled in the dirt like two animals. Léon's face was drenched in sweat, blood pouring from an ugly cut above his eye as she stood watching helplessly, her mouth dry with fear. Then, with a sob, she saw the hands groping for Léon's throat, giant muscles bulging and straining as they sought for a hold. The fingers moved, closing tightly, squeezing...

Léon drove his knee hard into the other's groin, twisting away as his opponent roared with pain. In one swift movement Léon was on his feet, his sword in his hand, plunging it deeply into the rolling figure on the ground. There was a moan and a hideous sucking sound, and then only Léon's raw breathing as he sheathed the bloodied sword and kicked the lifeless body over with his boot.

Almost immediately there came the frantic sound of a horse being mounted. Still breathing harshly Léon turned.

'I think not,' he said, catching hold of the horse. 'A long walk will cool your thirst for a burning.'

Half senseless with terror the man dismounted, staring at Léon like a rabbit at a fox.

'I loved your companion more,' Léon said contemptuously as the man backed away from him. 'At least he had the stomach for a fight.' He turned to Marietta. 'Which pleases you? The bay or the roan?'

'The bay,' Marietta said weakly.

He grinned, holding the stirrup for her. 'I judge it will take this craven coward the better part of the night and morning to reach Evray. Let's wish him good fortune. He'll need it. Wolves have a delicate partiality for witch-hunters, I'm told!'

His victim moaned in terror. Léon laughed, swinging up into his saddle and gathering the reins of the riderless horse with his own.

'Are we safe now?' Marietta asked as he slapped the rump of her horse into movement and cantered alongside. She glanced over her shoulder. The track was empty except for the cringing figure of the witch-hunter, the only movement the quivering of the boughs in their wake and the spiralling of leaves, silvered in the moonlight.

'Aye.' The generous mouth curved in a smile, white teeth flashing. 'Did you ever doubt it?'

She looked across at the bloodied, forceful young man beside her. 'No,' she said, dizzy with relief. 'I never doubted it.'

The wind had dropped and the night was fine and dry as they cantered at an easy pace beneath the soughing of the trees. Gradually the branches above their heads thinned and they could see the pale glimmer of the stars and the beginning of open country. Léon patted his horse's neck, feeling his coat rough and clammy with sweat. In a fold of the hills was the squat shape of a farmstead and he nodded across to it.

'A warm barn will take care of us for the rest of the night. My horse is tired.'

Marietta glanced over her shoulder doubtfully and Léon said: 'It will be mid-day before any news reaches Evray, and then I doubt that they'll give chase. Rest easy. We're safe enough.'

His confidence reassured her and she swung her horse off the road, following Léon across the fields. As he approached the darkened farm he dismounted, leading the animals quietly by the reins. There was the dull growl of a dog and Léon whistled softly, approaching the flattened ears and bristling fur with gentle words and outstretched hand. The dog sniffed round him suspiciously, and then the heavy tail wagged and the ears pricked as he licked Léon's boot.

'Saints alive,' Marietta whispered. 'What sort of a dog is that?'

'Like a woman,' Léon said carelessly, and pushed open the barn door.

It was pitch black inside, and strong with the smell of cow and horse. Holding her by the hand, he guided her through the darkness to the rough wood of a ladder. She climbed obediently, sinking with relief on to soft straw.

He kicked off his boots and unbuckled his sword, lying down beside her. The danger from which they had just escaped had heightened his senses and the memory of her body, firm and supple beneath his, was still fresh in his mind. He reached out for her confidently, his hand slipping inside her torn bodice as he rolled across her. He was rewarded by a stinging blow to his cheek and a knee brought up hard and high in his groin.

'Hell's light,' he gasped, letting go of her and doubling up in pain. 'What was that for?'

'For treating me like the dog,' Marietta said, her voice shaking with fury.

'But I've just saved your life!' he protested, incredulous at having his advances spurned.

'And does that give you the right to make free with me?' Marietta demanded, springing to her feet.

Léon's eyes had accustomed themselves to the dark and he could see the milky whiteness of a well-shaped breast as it

25

escaped from her torn bodice. Hastily she clutched at the remnants of tattered blue serge, holding the material tightly as she searched for the ladder.

'I would have thought it gave me the right to something,' Léon said reasonably. 'That ox of a witch-hunter nearly choked the light out of me.'

'And would have done so if I hadn't sunk my teeth into his thigh!' Marietta retorted tartly, continuing to search on her hands and knees for the elusive ladder.

'You'll knock it over doing that.' Léon watched her in growing amusement. 'I can make the jump easily, but I think you may find it a little difficult.'

The word she used would have done credit to a guardsman. Léon's grin widened.

'I'll make a bargain with you. I'll not seduce you if you promise to act sensibly and stop grovelling around the edge of an eight-foot drop and lie down and go to sleep.'

She hesitated.

'Oh, for goodness' sake,' Léon said exasperatedly. 'I'm not so desperate for female company that I need force myself where I'm not wanted.'

To prove his point he moved to the far side of the loft and resettled himself beneath the shutters.

Relieved at not having to brave the night

alone, Marietta returned, lying as far away from him as possible. Even at that distance Léon was uncomfortably aware of her body and of the intangible smell of fresh lavender. He closed his eyes determinedly and tried to sleep. A peasant girl could not possibly smell of lavender, especially a girl who had just fled miles through thick forest with a whole village at her heels. The tantalising fragrance continued to torment him, and he tossed restlessly. Despite his cloak and the straw he was still uncomfortably cold. There was a stifled sob and then another. He opened his eyes.

'Are you crying?'

'No.' The choking reply was a blatant lie.

He remembered the hideous flames from the funeral pyre.

'Is it because of your grandmother?'

There was no reply, only the sound of her weeping.

'The innkeeper said she was dead by the time they took her up the hill. The Inquisitor had a hollow victory. There's no need for you to cry.'

'There is! I loved her and now she's dead I have no one. No one at all.'

Léon was not used to situations he was not master of. Crying females usually made him impatient, but this one was crying for a real grief and not just the loss of a bauble or trinket. He rolled over, seeing the black shape of her figure, knees hugged high to her chest, her fists pressed against her mouth as she struggled to control her tears.

He reached out his arm, his fingers touching her lightly on the shoulder. This time she made no move to free herself from his touch.

'She was good, not bad. Good. There wasn't a cottage in Evray that didn't benefit from her medicines and ointments.'

Gently Léon took her in his arms, pulling her reassuringly against his chest, stroking her hair as she cried herself into a state of exhaustion. It was a strange feeling, rather like holding a child. Léon felt a wave of tenderness and mocked himself for a fool. His gesture of comfort was costing him dear. His collar of Chantilly lace had never been intended for use as a makeshift handkerchief, and he was going to look a shade less debonair in the morning.

Gradually her breathing eased, changing from harsh gasps to the deep rhythm of sleep. He eased her head from his shoulder, lying her on the straw, covering her with his cloak. Then, his body close to hers for warmth, he closed his eyes, secure in the knowledge that the scent of lavender had not been imagination but had come from her hair.

The rustle of cocks and hens woke him at dawn. Pale light seeped in from closed shutters. He opened them cautiously. The farmhouse was still quiet, which was just as well. He had no desire to explain their presence to a farmer who might be only too pleased to inform any who came looking for them that they had only recently left and were within easy distance.

There was a soft murmur as Marietta turned in her sleep. He glanced down at her and frowned. Saving her had given him the pleasure of a good fight, and her spirited rebuff of his advances the previous evening had amused him. But in the clear light of morning he wanted nothing more than to be speedily on his way to Elise, and the sleeping girl at his feet was an encumbrance he could have done without.

He nudged her gently with his foot and she awoke with a cry of fear, scrambling to her feet.

'It's all right,' he said reassuringly. 'You're safe, remember?'

It took a few seconds for her memory to return: for the fear in her eyes to die. The man before her with the slight frown on his face had saved her life. He was tall, with broad shoulders and lean hips, his clothes lavishly embellished with lace, his velvet cloak lined with jewel-coloured silk. Coal-black hair hung in riotous curls to his shoulders. His nose was strong and hawk-like; the mouth that laughed so easily, firm,

29

even harsh in repose. He looked like a man used to command. A man accustomed to getting his own way.

'Thank you for last night,' she said, suddenly aware of her bare feet and tattered gown.

He shrugged. 'It was nothing. A mere diversion.'

'It may have been nothing to you, monsieur! It was my Grandmother's death to me!'

'And nearly the death of me,' Léon returned drily. 'Perhaps you would favour me by wearing my cloak. As you so adamantly refused my attentions last night it seems unfair to stand before me half naked.'

Marietta glanced hurriedly down to where his eyes lingered admiringly. The blood rose in her cheeks as he threw his cloak carelessly around her shoulders.

'A pleasant sight, mademoiselle, but not when one has been forbidden to touch.'

He was laughing at her, and Marietta was not used to being laughed at. Her eyes glittered fiercely. They were thick-lashed and a brilliant green, the corners tilting tantalisingly upwards. Her face was too small and heartshaped for beauty, or at least the beauty that was fashionable at Versailles; it reminded Léon of a kitten he had once had when he was a boy. There was a smudge of dirt on her cheek and he felt an uncontrollable urge to wipe it away.

Before he could do so there came the distant sound of hoofbeats. He froze, listening intently. The drumming hooves came nearer and the blood drained from Marietta's face.

'Is it them?' Her eyes dilated with fear. 'Oh, what shall we do? Where can we hide?'

Léon seized his sword and crossed hastily to the half-open shutters. He could see them clearly. Three riders, and all heading unmistakably for the farmhouse.

'Is it them?' Marietta asked again.

'Aye, but only one fighting man amongst them. Unless our unwitting host is a force to reckon with.'

They were near enough to distinguish now and Léon could see the reedy-voiced man he had struck such terror into the previous night and the flapping black robes of the Inquisitor. Only the third man, roughly dressed and with a massive chest showing beneath his leather jerkin, was a stranger.

Marietta stifled a sob. 'They'll take me back to him. Back to the Inquisitor.'

At the thought of those glacial eyes in the cadaverous face Marietta's cheeks whitened so much that Léon thought she would faint with terror.

'Then they'll not have far to take you,' he said grimly, 'for he's not fifty yards away.'

31

'Holy Mary,' Marietta's lips moved soundlessly and Léon's fingers tightened on the hilt of his sword. Three against one was acceptable odds to the man known to Louis' troops as the Lion of Languedoc.

'Have you so little faith in me?' His eyes were bold and confident.

'No.' The feeling of dizziness passed. She gave him a shaky smile. 'What must we do?'

'For the moment, wait and see the sort of support our three friends are going to receive from our host.'

They were so near now that Marietta could hear the harsh breathing of the horses. The men's voices sounded loud and clear in the barn. She froze, not daring to move an inch, terrified of rustling the straw on which they had slept. Below, on the floor of the barn, Léon's horse moved restlessly and Marietta felt as if her heart had ceased to beat.

If they could hear the horses... If they should suspect...

'The place looks deserted, Your Honour.' The thin voice was unmistakable.

'Deserted, my foot,' the Inquisitor said harshly. 'Pierre Duroq has always been an idle layabout. A good whipping would soon set him to rights! Well, what are you waiting for, dolt? Knock him up. Break down the door if necessary. By the Mass, if I find he so much as gave that strumpet a drink of water I'll have two fires on Valais Hill tonight, not one!'

'Yes, Your Honour.' Trembling visibly he did as he was bid, hammering at the door till a shutter above flew open and a bleary-eyed, red-faced man spat volubly on him.

'What the devil do you think you're doing? Can't a decent man lie abed in his own house?' He saw the straight-backed figure of the Inquisitor and the words died on his lips.

'We're seeking a witch, and have good reason to believe she came this way.'

'There's been no witch here,' Pierre Duroq said hurriedly. 'I'm a loyal, decent citizen, not a harbourer of witches.'

'Then you'll have no objection if we search your property?'

'None at all.' Pierre Duroq scrambled into his shirt and breeches while the Inquisitor looked speculatively around him. The barn was the only place of any substance.

Léon moved stealthily, hauling up the rickety ladder to the loft in which they had sought sanctuary.

'But that won't stop them,' Marietta whispered.

'Sshh.' Softly he called his horse till it stood directly beneath him. 'Can you jump on to his back from here?' he asked quietly.

Marietta swallowed. 'Yes. I think so. But you…'

'Never mind me. I have my own plans,' and the gleam in his eyes showed he was contemplating them with a measure of enjoyment. 'Don't move until I tell you, then jump on to Saracen and dig your heels in.'

The barn door opened, letting in a flood of pale morning light.

'There's the horse!' the high-pitched voice quavered excitedly.

The burly figure at the Inquisitor's side drew a fine honed knife from his belt, approaching stealthily. Hardly daring to breathe Marietta watched him from her hiding-place as he kicked at the straw bales in the far recesses of the barn. The Inquisitor moved his horse slowly forward.

'Not a thing.' The final bale was kicked over in disgust.

The Inquisitor paused, his horse parallel with Léon's, eyeing the dusty floor thoughtfully. The marks where the ladder had stood showed clearly.

'We have them,' he said softly.

Before his henchman could reach his side he raised his eyes to the loft and immediately Léon jumped.

Marietta gave a cry of alarm as the muscled figure, the knife held high, leapt forward. But Léon had landed neatly behind the Inquisitor. While the horse whinnied in fear at receiving a second rider so unceremoniously, Léon wrenched the Inquisitor's hand high between his shoulder blades, his free hand holding a knife quite as deadly as that of his adversary. And it was pointed directly at the Inquisitor's throat.

'Not so hasty, friend. Not if you want your master here to live to see another day. Call him off!' This last remark was made to his victim, and Marietta could see the knife-blade break the flesh and a trickle of blood run down the Inquisitor's neck.

'Do as he says.' The Inquisitor's voice was hoarse.

'Tell him to throw the knife in the loft.'

The black-robed arm was moved another inch higher till he did as he was bid. Marietta moved hurriedly to one side as the knife flew upwards, burying itself in the straw. Feverishly she retrieved it, putting it between her teeth as Léon shouted:

'Jump and ride like the Devil!'

'Stop her, you fool!' the Inquisitor cried as Marietta leapt on to Saracen, showing a display of long slender legs that only Léon was in a position to appreciate.

'If they do, you'll never live to enjoy it.'

The two men paused, Léon's previous adversary nothing loth at having a valid excuse for not showing his mettle, and Marietta dug in her heels. Saracen bolted for the open doors, knocking the terrified Pierre Duroq to the ground as he hurried to see what his unwelcome guests had found.

'And now for a little ride,' Léon said to his captive. 'The countryside is at its best this time of morning,' and grinning broadly, the knife still in one hand, the reins in the other, Léon dug in his spurs and galloped out into the sunlight after Marietta.

A better man would have immediately unseated him, but Léon knew the cowardice of a man who ordered others to do his torturing and burning. The stiff-backed figure in front of him remained rigid as Léon raced down over open meadows that led to the forest and the path, the gap between himself and Marietta narrowing every minute. She turned, and on seeing the black robes flying in the wind screamed in fear; then, seeing Léon's broad shoulders and the flash of steel she reined in her horse until he drew alongside her, her face radiant.

'You did it! Oh, I thought they had killed you!'

'It would take more than two lily-livered apologies for men and one with no brains to do that,' Léon said contemptuously.

'You'll roast in the fires of hell for this.' The Inquisitor's finely drawn features were pinched and white, his mouth such a thin line that it had almost disappeared entirely.

'For my sake, I hope not,' Léon replied grimly. 'I find your company here on earth bad enough without meeting you in the

Hereafter!' And he urged the horse to a gallop, the green of the trees closing in above their heads.

When he had put several miles between themselves and the farmhouse he reined in, ordering his shaking victim to dismount.

'What are you going to do with him?' Marietta asked fearfully. 'Kill him?'

Léon looked down at the ashen face and terrified eyes. Gone was the ice-cold authority; only the hate remained.

'I wouldn't demean myself,' he said easily, sending the Inquisitor stumbling backwards as the toe of his yellow boot connected with the black-robed shoulder. 'I've killed many men, but only in battle. This one isn't worthy to be called a man – let him crawl back to his hole as best he may.'

Another thrust of his boot and the Inquisitor was sent sprawling. Léon grinned across at Marietta.

'The sooner we put some distance between us and Evray the better. What say you?' he asked as Saracen pawed the ground impatiently.

'I say yes,' Marietta said, pushing a tangle of copper-coloured curls away from her face. Where they were going she did not know – nor did she care. She slapped Saracen's rump lightly and galloped after him down the dust-blown track.

Chapter Two

She only looked behind her once. In the distance Valais Hill rose hazily above the sea of trees and she reined in Saracen, staring fixedly at it through a mist of tears. Léon wheeled the Inquisitor's horse around, cantering back to her. As he reached her she lifted her chin and squared her slender shoulders. The past was past. Only the future mattered.

A strong, well-shaped hand reached across and gripped hers. She squeezed it tightly, and as their eyes met she saw they were not as dark as she had previously thought, but a warm, golden brown. There was no trace of the mocking smile or lazy amusement that so infuriated her. Instead he was looking at her with understanding, and she was grateful for it.

She smiled. 'It was one last goodbye. I shan't cry again, I promise you.'

'For my collar's sake, I'm glad.'

Marietta looked at the crumpled lace that had been so immaculate the previous evening and a faint tinge heightened her cheeks.

'Did I do that? I don't remember.'

'It's no matter,' Léon said graciously, reflecting that if his valet at court had presented him with such a sad apology for adornment he would have had his hide.

'I'll make you another one.'

'Not like this,' Léon said as they resumed their ride. 'This collar is of the best Chantilly lace.'

'Anyone can make Chantilly,' Marietta said disrespectfully. 'My grandmother was a Venetian and Venetians make the best lace in the world.'

What she said was true, and Léon was suitably impressed. The lace on his bucket-top boots had cost him a fortune. At least he need have no fears about her future. A lace-maker would always eat.

'And do you make lace in the Venetian fashion?'

She laughed. 'Yes. And keep it secret.'

'Then you'll have no trouble in making a living.'

'No.' She felt suddenly deflated. Life had been lonely enough these past ten years, but there had always been her grandmother for company. Now there would be nobody. Despite the warmth of the sun she shivered.

'Sometimes it helps to talk.'

'There's nothing to talk about.' Marietta said as the road curved down through fertile orchards.

Remembering the events of the past few

hours Léon felt she was making something of an understatement. 'Why do the men of Evray say you're a witch?' he asked curiously.

'Because they are fools.'

He laughed. 'I'll not argue with you there. But if you're not a witch, who and what are you?'

'Marietta Riccardi, and I've told you what I am. I'm a lacemaker.' Her pride in her art was unmistakable.

'And what were you doing in Evray? Evray isn't a lacemaking village.'

'My grandmother was too weak to travel further.'

He waited silently and after a little while she said: 'As a child we lived in Venice, but my mother was French and these last ten years we lived in Paris.'

She no longer saw the sun-filled road before them: only the beautiful city of canals and palaces that had been her childhood home. 'When first she and then my father died my grandmother wanted to return to Venice. She fell sick in Evray and so we remained there, never accepted, always foreigners. Her skill at making medicines from herbs, instead of winning us friends, made us enemies. They said it was witchcraft that gave her the ability to cure fevers and chills. And that witches had to die.' Her hands tightened on the reins. 'It was all *his*

41

fault. Before he came the people were grateful enough to her. It was he who put thoughts of witchcraft into their stupid minds.'

'Him?' Léon asked intrigued. 'Who?'

She shrugged her shoulders helplessly. 'I don't know. He came late at night when I was asleep. He wanted a poison and my grandmother refused to give it to him. He said she would either give him the formula for it or burn. When I heard his threats and my grandmother's protests I rushed into the room, but he was already outside and mounting his horse. All that I could see was that he was a man of quality. A nobleman with beringed hands.'

Léon remembered the jewelled hand of the man who had ridden into the inn yard, demanding torches and more horses. He frowned. 'Why should a man of substance resort to asking a harmless old woman for a poison? Poisons can be procured easily enough.'

'My grandmother was an Italian,' Marietta said simply.

She had no need to say more. It was the Italians who had first elevated the crime of poisoning to a fine art. Catherine de' Medici had brought the evil with her when she arrived in France to be the bride of Henri II. Marie de' Medici, on her marriage to Henri IV, had continued to spread the evil.

The Borgias, the Medicis, all were poisoners and all were Italians, or were believed to be.

'Are you trying to tell me that your grandmother was skilled in arts other than lacemaking and the making of medicines to cure chills?'

The full, soft lips closed tight. 'My grandmother was good,' she repeated firmly. 'She never harmed anybody.'

'But she could if she had wanted to?'

Her eyes met his, bold and unafraid. 'She had great knowledge and she never abused it. And neither shall I.' And with that she dug her heels into Saracen's side and galloped ahead of him to where plane trees lined the road, giving welcome shade.

'Well, I'll be damned,' Léon said beneath his breath as he urged his own horse to catch up with her. If anyone else had told him of a mysterious nobleman visiting an obscure cottage in an even obscurer village in search of a rare poison, he would have dismissed it as moonshine. But Marietta's words held the ring of truth. And she had insinuated that she, too, knew the secret their unknown visitor had been after. Was that why he had been so keen to capture Marietta Riccardi?

He shook his head in an effort to clear it. He was thinking like a peasant. No doubt the old woman had been well versed in the use of herbs, and herbs could be harmful to the body as well as beneficial, and any local seigneur would count as a nobleman in the eyes of a peasant girl like Marietta. That was all there was to it. Nothing more.

He drew alongside her, opened his mouth to assure her that her nobleman was no one more important or mysterious than a local landowner, and decided against it. Gullible she might be, but she certainly had courage and did not deserve his ridicule.

The sunlight glinted on the copper-coloured curls that hung in a wild tangle around her face and shoulders, turning them into a fiery nebula. She rode well, and that in itself was a curiosity; barefoot village girls had no right to look at ease on a horse as powerful as Saracen. She held herself with an unconscious grace that many a lady at court would have envied. Yet not one of them would have jumped the terrifying distance from the hayloft to Saracen's back. The mere thought of it would have given them the vapours. The girl at his side had not even murmured a protest. Her gown was muddied, her bodice so torn that even despite his cloak that she still wore round her shoulders, he could see her breasts rising and falling temptingly as Saracen cantered over the rutted path. With great difficulty he turned his head.

Marietta noticed with relief that the countryside was unfamiliar to her, and that therefore Evray was a good distance behind. A stream crossed their path and Léon swung from his horse, taking bread and cheese from Saracen's saddlebag and sitting on the bank. Marietta joined him, taking the bread gratefully as Léon halved it, not protesting as he gave her the larger portion of the cheese.

Léon drank deeply from the fast-moving water, wondering how long it had been since she had last had food and wishing he had remembered the bread and cheese earlier.

Behind him Marietta lay down, her eyes closed as she enjoyed the heat of the sun on her face.

Léon turned, watching her through half-closed eyes. It had been ten years since he had made love to a village girl. She had been rosy-cheeked with ample breasts and square, capable hands more suited to milking than love-making. She had been his first conquest and he remembered her with affection. Since then his lady-loves had been painted and powdered and dressed in silk and satins. Francine Beauvoir bathed in milk and even her shoes were diamond-studded, yet she hadn't half Marietta's beauty. Or her spirit.

Sensing his intent gaze, she opened her eyes. He lay beside her, propping himself up on his elbow as he gazed down at her. She

45

stiffened at his nearness and he laughed. 'Don't worry. I'm not going to make any assaults on your virtue.'

'Then what are you going to do?' Marietta asked, her heart pounding at the purposeful expression in the amber eyes.

Slowly he traced the outline of her mouth with his finger.

'After risking my life twice to save you, I think the least you can do is reward me with a kiss,' and he bent his head to hers, ignoring her initial protest, kissing her deeply. Marietta's hand pushed vainly at him and then slid imperceptibly upwards and around his neck as his mouth seared hers. Then, all too soon, he released her, saying lightly:

'Your debts are now settled, mademoiselle.'

No one had ever held her like that before. The men of Evray had pawed at her and been dealt with by a sharp box on the ear. Not one of them was worthy to touch the hem of her gown, her grandmother had told her that in no uncertain terms and the rumours of her grandmother's mysterious powers had been enough to see that she hadn't been troubled further. She was the daughter of Pietro Riccardi and her grandmother had told her always to remember it. Marietta had, but her grandmother had not warned her about a young man with powerful shoulders and lean hips; with dancing eyes and a laughing mouth and hair thick and soft beneath her fingers.

'We must be on our way.'

Already he was striding back towards his horse, and Marietta followed dazedly, not realising that he was furiously angry with himself.

Marietta's kiss had inflamed him so that it had taken all of his not inconsiderable self-control to restrain himself from making love to her. A country girl who, despite her protests the previous night, was no doubt as free with her favours as every other woman. Certainly she was showing very little resistance to him now! Only Elise was different. If it hadn't been for Marietta he would have been at Chatonnay by nightfall. Now it would be tomorrow at the earliest, and coupled with that was the knowledge that he had been on the verge of breaking his vow of fidelity.

Léon's experience of women had been gained in the brothels of Spain and in Louis' court at Versailles. It had convinced him that all women were wantons who would give themselves freely for baubles and pretty clothes. Only Elise was different and that was why he loved her. She was pure as the driven snow, shy and gentle, blushing at his slightest touch.

For years he had felt physically sick

47

whenever he had thought of her in Sainte-Beauve's bed. Now at last she was free and he had sent word that he was coming to marry her. The boy who had left Chatonnay with not two *livres* to rub together was returning with more wealth than any man for leagues around. The château that his mother still lived in would soon be returned to its former glory, making a fitting home for Elise and for their future children. Louis had been insistent that he return to court but Léon had no intention of doing so. He had had his bellyful of court life with its light morals and sinister intrigues. He wanted nothing more than to supervise his southern estates, rearing his sons in the countryside he loved. In a land smelling of wine and garlic and not the cloying perfumes of Paris and Versailles.

Marietta, happily unaware of the direction of his thoughts, cantered along by his side as they passed fields where peasants tilled the land and entered a bustling village, noisy with playing children. The women watched them curiously, noting Marietta's bare feet and the richness of Léon's doublet and boots, continuing with their spinning and speculating amongst themselves.

'Are you hungry?' Léon asked, as they left the tiled roofs and dusty lanes of the village behind them.

'Yes.' The bread and cheese had been

welcome but had only served to take the edge off her appetite. She looked hopefully at his saddlebag, and despite himself he smiled. She was an engaging baggage and it wasn't her fault if her presence disturbed him.

'I've nothing else with me. We'll soon be in Toulouse. We'll stop there and have a decent meal.'

The sandy road wound on between fields of yellow maize and at last Toulouse appeared on the horizon, towers and steeples gleaming beneath a brilliant blue sky.

In a blessedly short space of time they were riding through the main gate into the noisy confusion of market day. Countryfolk from far and wide had gathered to sell their produce, and the narrow cobbled streets were crowded with jostling farmers and pannier-hung donkeys. Léon forced his way through carts and wagons, sheep and cows, to the inn yard. The groom, noticing the scratches and grazes on Marietta's legs and the muddied hem of her dress, watched curiously as Léon helped her from the saddle. Marietta, seeing his glance, wrapped Léon's cloak tightly around her shoulders, determined not to shame him more by showing her tattered bodice.

The landlord set two mugs of frothing ale before them and served them a roast of mutton and steaming plates of beans and cabbage. Marietta ate ravenously and the strong ale went a little way to sweetening Léon's temper.

'You know everything about me,' she said, when her plate was clean. 'My name, where I come from, everything. I know nothing about you at all. Not even,' she felt suddenly shy, 'not even your name.'

'That's easily rectified,' Léon said, his hunger satisfied and his thirst slaked. 'Léon de Villeneuve. I've spent the last six years alternately fighting for Louis and attending him at court.'

'At Versailles?' Marietta's eyes widened.

He nodded. 'Now I'm on my way home to Chatonnay.'

'Do they have lacemakers in Chatonnay?' Marietta asked tentatively.

'No, more's the pity,' he added, thinking of the long journey he would have to make to purchase lace fine enough for Elise's gowns.

'Is it to Chatonnay that we're riding?'

'It's to Chatonnay that *I'm* riding,' he corrected.

Her face whitened. 'I thought I was to travel with you?'

'Away from Evray,' Léon agreed, helping himself to apple tart. 'And I'll give you the horse and a gold piece when we part.'

'I don't want your gold!' Marietta said thickly. 'I thought that…' She faltered, the colour rushing into her cheeks.

He said bluntly, 'I ride to Chatonnay to marry.'

She stared unbelievingly at him, the blood drumming in her ears. 'Then you shouldn't have treated me as a whore!'

'God's grace, I only kissed you!' Léon protested defensively.

Pie and plate were flung across his face.

'Hell and the Devil!' Léon's temper snapped. He seized her wrist, dragging her from the table as pastry and fruit clung to his cheek, dripping down on to his doublet. 'I should have left you to burn!'

She clawed at his face wildly, and the landlord came running in just in time to see Léon force a struggling Marietta firmly across his knee and slap her resoundingly. The landlord grinned, crossing his arms to watch at his leisure. No doubt the wench had asked for it. She'd made a sorry state of her escort's doublet with his wife's apple tart, and there was blood oozing from scratchmarks down his face.

'That,' Léon said, his hand coming down hard, 'is for having me struggle through bush and thicket to catch you in the first place! *This,'* his hand came down to a piercing scream, 'is for my having to gallop my horse half to death! And *this!'* The landlord winced. 'Is for having me half strangled by that oaf of a witch-hunter!'

He let her go so sharply that she tumbled to the floor, giving the landlord a pleasing view of long legs and heaving breasts. She scrambled to her feet, snatched the mug of ale and flung it full in Léon's face before darting for the door and the street.

'Hell's light!' Léon cursed, wiping the foam from his eyes.

The innkeeper chuckled. 'I reckon you are better off without her. That hair colouring always denotes temper, and she's got it in plenty.'

Léon agreed fervently. The landlord went for another tankard of ale to replace the one now soaking his handsomely-dressed customer as Léon removed as much of the pie and fruit as possible. She'd left his cloak behind, which meant she was walking the streets of the town exposing herself tantalisingly to the general gaze. Léon grinned. It would take a brave man to take advantage of her. Whore indeed! She didn't know the meaning of the word.

For the first time it occurred to Léon that she was, just possibly, a virgin. He shrugged. It was none of his affair. He was better off without her – she was too disturbing a companion for a man on the verge of matrimony. The innkeeper set his tankard down and then hurried away as a fresh influx of visitors burst noisily through the door.

It was doubtful if Léon would have

recognised the face in the light of day, but the huge diamond on the black-gauntleted hand was unmistakable.

'Food and drink, and quick about it,' its owner said curtly to the innkeeper, and then to one of his companions. 'Of course she's here. This is the nearest town of any substance. We'll have her before nightfall.'

It was an elegant face. The fair hair carefully coiffured, the moustache and pointed beard immaculately trimmed, and with light blue eyes cold as steel.

Léon left his ale untouched, striding out into the yard for his horse.

'He's not through feeding yet, sir...' the groom began, but Léon wasn't listening. He was already outside the yard trotting briskly down a street thick with chattering peasant women and street traders. None of them was disposed to move out of his way. The sun was shining, the stalls were heavy with red apples and golden pears, plums and pumpkins and great bunches of summer flowers. Farmers and shepherds seeking an afternoon's entertainment, thronged the street, blocking his way.

He could see the flame of her hair as it whisked out of sight down an alleyway and he cursed at the shawled women, their overflowing baskets on their arms, who prevented him from giving chase. It seemed that every housewife in the district was doing her shopping, and that every cat and dog and shouting child in the vicinity had nothing better to do than stand in the way of his horse and refuse to move. Losing the last shreds of his patience, he forced his way through relentlessly, getting plenty of abuse for his pains and upsetting a large basket of carrots so that they spilled across the cobbles, much to the glee of the children who snatched at them greedily.

The alley was so narrow that there was scarce room for his horse. Marietta gave a cry and ran faster, hurtling past a surprised pedlar as shutter after shutter flew open so that the occupants of the houses could see what the commotion was about.

'*Let me go! Let me go!*' she shrieked as he galloped up to her, his hand catching the flying mane of hair.

'I wish to God I could,' Léon said sincerely, swinging down from his horse and pinioning her against the wall. 'But you'll come with me till we're further from Evray *and* take the horse and gold. I do not want your death on my conscience.'

He was pressed close against her, breathing harshly, his eyes blazing. Savagely he grabbed her wrist, uncomfortably aware of the ribald comments of the pedlar.

'They're at the inn looking for you. You stand no chance unless you leave immediately.'

She needed no more persuading. He thrust Saracen's reins into her hands.

'I'm going back for the other horse. Wait for me here in the alleyway.'

'What if they come while you are gone?'

At the sight of her frightened face he forgot that she had just ruined his clothes, made a fool of him in public and brought him twice within an inch of death.

'They won't,' he said confidently, and to his surprise and hers kissed her full on the mouth before striding back through the crowds for the horse.

Marietta raised a hand to her bruised lips, her heart racing, but not with fear. She could never be afraid if Léon was with her. Why had he kissed her? Only minutes ago he had admitted he was about to marry. Did a kiss mean so little to him? The pressure of his lips on hers still burned. It hadn't felt like a kiss of no consequence. She stared after him, her cheeks scarlet.

Léon swore at himself for a fool. By the time he reached the inn yard he had convinced himself that he had kissed her merely to comfort her and that it had given him no carnal satisfaction at all. It wasn't an argument that would have stood up to scrutiny, and knowing that he thrust it to the back of his mind and concentrated on getting the horse out of the inn yard before either he or it were recognised.

Inside the crowded inn he could see the fair-headed man standing impatiently, a chicken leg in one hand, a tankard of ale in the other. It wouldn't be long before he resumed his search.

Léon tipped the stable boy handsomely and forced his way through the crowded streets to where Marietta anxiously waited. At the sight of him, broad-shouldered and sitting his horse with careless grace, Marietta's heart skipped a beat. Hastily she mounted Saracen, wincing at the discomfort that sitting gave her. She wondered if he would have treated the girl he was to marry in such a cavalier manner, beating her in public. She doubted it, and felt a wave of jealousy.

Léon was too preoccupied to notice Marietta's physical discomfort. The man he had seen at the inn was no ordinary witch-hunter. If he would go to the trouble of travelling so far in search of Marietta he would go further. But why? Not for the mere pleasure of burning her. Perhaps her grandmother had passed on to her secrets that were of value – but if she had now was not the time to ask about them.

The street-seller grabbed his basket of carrots protectively as they rode by, glad to see the back of them, while the rest of the populace took a few moments from a busy day to gaze appraisingly at the well-set young man with the unruly curls and the maid with slanting green eyes riding straight-backed by his side.

With the city walls behind them, Léon and Marietta rode their horses to the limit, only when it was impossible for their mounts to continue further did they stop. The sun was beginning to sink: soon it would be dusk. Léon leant his back against a solitary tree and wiped the perspiration from his brow.

'We'll not be able to travel any further for a good while. The horses need rest.'

'So do I,' Marietta said, sinking weakly beside him. Some yards away the horses grazed by the flower-filled banks of the Garonne, the sound of the rushing water soothing to Marietta's ears. 'Are we safe now? Will they follow us?'

'They won't follow us if they didn't see us,' Léon said practically. 'They're intent on searching the town. That should occupy them until tomorrow and a little longer, with luck.'

'What then? Will they come this way?'

'Further into Languedoc? I doubt it. You're safe now.'

'How did the Inquisitor get another horse so quickly?' Marietta asked. 'We left him miles from anywhere.'

'It wasn't the Inquisitor who was searching for you. It was another man – the one I saw demanding more torches and horses in the search for you at Evray.'

'Another man?' Marietta looked at him blankly.

'Young and fair-haired and richly dressed.' She paled. 'That must be *him*. The man who came to my grandmother to demand her secret.'

'Why should he be searching for you?'

Marietta stood up and walked slowly the few yards to the bank of the river. 'Because I know all my grandmother's secrets. He's searching for me so that I will tell him what he most wants to know.'

'But poisons are commonplace.' Léon protested. 'I was there myself when Madame, the Princess Henrietta of England, was poisoned at court by having diamond powder sprinkled on her strawberries instead of sugar.'

Marietta gave a little laugh. 'She may have been poisoned, but it wasn't with diamond powder.'

'How would you know?' Léon asked amused. 'You weren't at court and I was.'

'Particles of diamond powder or ground glass are sharp enough to damage the stomach, but the Princess Henrietta would have been conscious of them on her food before she swallowed. Such things are for suicides, not murders.'

Her words held conviction. Léon tried again.

'Then it could have been the chicory water that was poisoned. She no sooner put the cup down than she was in agony.'

Marietta looked at him pityingly. 'The only poisons that would act so speedily are mercury salt and oil of vitriol, and both of those would have burnt her mouth. It's my guess the Princess' death was due to natural causes.'

'Then you're the only person in France who thinks so,' Léon said good-naturedly. 'Though I still don't see why our fine-feathered friend should seek out you and your grandmother with such determination. In Paris a visit to any one of a hundred alchemists would give him all the poisons he desires.'

'You don't understand,' Marietta said, returning and sitting at his side. 'It wasn't the secret of poison alone that he wanted. It was something much rarer.' She paused. 'My grandmother knew the secret of protection against poison. That was what he was after.'

'There isn't one,' Léon said firmly. 'I've been at court long enough to know that. Anyone with that secret would make a fortune!'

Marietta gave a sad smile. 'Exactly, and that is why my grandmother was murdered.'

Léon stared at her. 'You're not telling me that your grandmother knew of a drug to make a man immune to poison?'

She nodded. 'That's why he searches for me. There can be no other reason.'

Léon's black brows drew together sharply. Paris was rife with talk of astronomy, alchemy and sorcery, and it was dangerous talk.

'If she did know, it's best not spoken of.'

A deep purple haze crept over the lonely countryside. He sighed. There was no shelter in sight and the horses were exhausted.

'We must sleep here till first light.'

She nodded acquiescence, lying down beside him as darkness fell. His cloak was not sufficient to cover them both, especially as he had left a prudent two-foot gap between his body and hers. He sighed again. Prudence would have to go to the winds. He couldn't freeze to death. He moved nearer her, slipping his arm around her shoulders, saying: 'It's too cold to sleep apart.'

She made no protest as he drew her into the circle of his arms, so close that she could feel the beating of his heart against hers. She covered his hand with her small one, wishing that he had not felt it necessary to explain away his gesture as a practicality. Wishing he would kiss her again, as he had in the alleyway.

For the second night Léon fell asleep with the faint smell of lavender sweetening his dreams. Her closeness gave him a ridiculous sense of pleasure. He told himself it was because he was lonely for Elise and strove to think of blonde hair and shy, violet-blue eyes instead of flashing green ones that were as easily roused to anger as to laughter. He failed, and comforted himself with the thought that it did not matter. Tomorrow their ways would part. He would never see her again.

Marietta found that it was warmer if she put her arms around Léon's waist and rested her head on his broad chest, and Léon saw no reason to object to such a pleasing arrangement.

Chapter Three

Marietta half opened her eyes, a ray of sunlight warm on her face, Léon's head heavy on her breast. Tentatively she fingered the dark curls, wondering if he powdered them when at court. He would have no need of a wig. The thick hair, shoulder-length, sprang pleasurably beneath her palm.

Léon half awoke, feeling the warmth of her body beneath his cheek. For a fleeting minute he thought himself in a Spanish brothel as his hand tightened around a hand-span waist. His eyes half-opened, narrow with desire, and he bent his head to kiss her. Instead of the anonymity of a painted and rouged face he saw green eyes he remembered only too well. He recoiled as if he had been struck.

'God's truth! What kind of strumpet are you?'

'I'm not a strumpet,' Marietta said furiously, scrambling to her feet.

'Then you're fast turning into one!' Unsatisfied desire made him harsh.

'It was *you* who was forcing your attentions on *me!*' Marietta pointed out as she mounted Saracen, trying to hide her humiliation.

'God forbid!' Léon strode over to the Inquisitor's horse. 'It was thanks to you that I had to spend the night in the open instead of in a comfortable bed. I was doing nothing more than keeping warm.'

'By putting your hand in my bodice?' Marietta asked scathingly.

An angry flush heightened his cheeks as he vaulted into his saddle.

'If I did so, rest assured I was asleep and not conscious of it,' he said cruelly. 'I'm on my way to marry a woman I've loved for years. It's hardly likely I would molest the peasant girls I pass *en route!*'

'I can't speak for the others, monsieur,' Marietta said sarcastically, 'but you certainly tried to molest me!'

'One kiss,' Léon scoffed, 'and an accidental kiss at that.'

Marietta trembled with fury.

'You should think yourself lucky to have gained so much. I'm a Riccardi, not a simple village girl to be tumbled in the grass by anyone who pleases!'

'For the last time, mademoiselle, I do *not* please!'

'Good, because your attentions, conscious or otherwise, are decidedly unwelcome!'

'Then good day, before my very proximity should bring on a fever,' Léon retorted witheringly. Angrily, they glared at each other from their mounts.

Marietta felt a surge of tears that she couldn't control. Before Léon could see them, she dug her heels in Saracen's side and galloped headlong away from him. At the sound of pounding hooves behind her she urged the horse faster.

'Oh, no you don't!' Léon's hand reached across for the reins, and at his master's order to halt. Saracen duly obeyed, whilst Marietta kept her head firmly averted as she dashed away her tears with the back of her hand.

'That horse,' Léon said, his voice dangerously quiet, 'happens to be mine.'

'Then take him!' Marietta leapt to the ground, staring up at him with her hands on her hips as if the loss of a horse miles from anywhere was only the merest inconvenience. She was blissfully unaware that without Léon's cloak she might as well have been naked from the waist upwards. Léon was aware of it, and as suddenly as his anger had been aroused it fled. He threw back his head and roared with laughter. She had hardly a rag to her back and she was looking at him, Léon de Villeneuve, the Lion of Languedoc, as haughtily as Francine Beauvoir would have looked at her lowest menial.

His laughter did nothing to improve Marietta's temper. As he showed no inclination to leave his present mount and had just appropriated Saracen, she swung on her heel, walking with her head held high, God alone knew where.

'That way lies the sea,' a deep timbred voice called after her enlighteningly.

She clenched her fists and altered direction.

'That way is to the mountains.'

He was riding his horse at a walking pace behind her. She could feel Saracen's breath on the nape of her neck. Her nails dug deep into her palms.

'And that way is a good day's ride before you would find so much as a cottage.'

'Then you'd better be on your way,' she retorted tartly. 'The morning's half spent already.'

'So it is,' Léon agreed affably. 'Get on your horse. I'll keep to my promise and not leave you until we reach somewhere you can stay.'

'*Your* horse, not mine!' Marietta kept on walking, not trusting herself to look at him.

'I would have thought the ground very painful to bare feet,' he continued conversationally.

Marietta bit back the word that rose to her lips. It was not one her grandmother would have wished her to use.

Léon, reflecting that at this pace he would never reach Chatonnay, swung from the saddle and, before Marietta realised his intention, spanned her waist with his hands

66

and lifted her on to Saracen's back. She tensed herself to spring defiantly once more to the ground and Léon's eyes held hers, the sun-bronzed face uncompromising.

'If you do, rest assured I shall leave you. I've wasted enough time already,' and he rode away from her at a gallop.

Marietta paused fractionally. She had a horse again. She could ride in another direction: to the mountains or the sea. He was already some distance away from her and showed not the slightest sign of turning to see if she was behind him. His threat to leave her had been no idle one. She had not the slightest doubt that he *would* leave her in this sun-baked wilderness without a second thought. And only yesterday she had been fool enough to respond to his kiss! Her cheeks burned with humiliation as she dug her heels in Saracen's side and raced unwillingly after him.

Léon, aware of the loss of pride that following him had cost her, remained sensitively silent as they cantered across a treeless landscape striped with vineyards. On their left the Garonne shone golden in the sun and they slowed their horses to a canter as the heat increased.

'It's very beautiful here,' Marietta said, unable to hold on to her anger any longer.

Léon's mouth softened. He loved Languedoc fiercely.

'It's a welcome change from Versailles.'

'Don't you like court life?' Marietta asked curiously.

Léon reflected on the beautiful and loose-moralled ladies who had made his life so pleasant over the last few years. Of the balls and banquets, the hunts and spectacles. Just when it had begun to pall he wasn't quite sure, but even before he had received news of Elise's widowhood he had known that he would leave. The fawning servility of the nobles vying for the King's attention sickened him. As a favourite of Louis, Léon had been besieged by those hoping to use him as a stepping-stone to the King's presence. He had been offered bribes of money and other bribes, for the noblemen of Versailles thought nothing of offering their wives' amorous services in return for a good word to the King from Léon. And the ladies had been nothing loth. Léon had spurned them as contemptuously as the gifts of money, and in doing so had made himself many enemies.

He had been uncaring. He had been at Versailles at Louis' special request, and because his Sovereign was a shrewd judge of men. The Lion of Languedoc was no sycophant. He had earned his nickname on the battlefields, and even Louvois, Secretary of State for War, valued his judgment. Louis had given him leave to return to Chatonnay and marry, ordering him and his wife to return to court immediately.

Léon had no intention of obeying his King's command. He was sure that once he had left Versailles Louis would forget him, surrounded as he was by so many others eager for his favours. He would be able to retire to the obscurity of Chatonnay and live life as he chose, his own man and not at another's beck and call, even if that other were the most powerful king in Christendom.

He said none of this to Marietta, merely saying a curt 'no' and continuing to ride, wondering if he would make Chatonnay by nightfall. In another few hours Elise would be in his arms. Six long years of waiting would be over...

'Is it true that Madame de Montespan has replaced La Villière in the King's affections?'

Léon's eyes darkened. 'What do you know of La Villière or Madame de Montespan?'

Marietta was pleased at having taken him aback with her knowledge.

'News of the King's loves reaches even into the countryside.'

'Not to Evray it doesn't,' Léon said grimly, reining in his horse and catching hold of her reins also. 'Madame de Montespan's name is still not known outside court. Who spoke to you of her?'

Marietta was beginning to regret her careless words. His face was formidable when he was angry. The lines from nose to mouth that deepened so beguilingly in laughter were now harsh and uncompromising.

She said nervously, 'I don't remember. It was just gossip.'

'Don't play me for a fool.' A strong brown hand grasped hers so tightly that she cried out in pain. 'How do you come to know so much about the happenings at court?'

Marietta's temporary feeling of goodwill towards him vanished.

'I told you before, but you chose not to believe me! I'm not just a simple peasant girl. I'm a Riccardi!'

'And do the Riccardis go to court?' Léon asked mockingly, his eyes lingering on her tattered dress.

Marietta would have slapped his face if her hand had been free and knowing it Léon's grasp tightened still further. 'No!' She spat at him. 'The court comes to the Riccardis!'

He laughed mirthlessly. 'You mean the man who searches for you?'

'He and others!'

Léon let go of her wrist, flinging it away from him. 'Then if they did it was to no good purpose!'

'None at all,' Marietta agreed, her eyes flashing. 'My grandmother never gave anyone anything that would cause harm.'

'And do you expect me to believe that noblemen from the court of Louis XIV travelled to Evray?' he asked, a contemptuous smile twisting his mouth.

'Not Evray. Paris. We lived in the shadow of the Pont-Neuf, near the rue Beauregard.'

Léon's eyebrows drew together sharply. He had heard of a woman in the rue Beauregard, a sybil all Paris flocked to hear. Not Marietta's grandmother, certainly, for La Voisin was no old woman trying to reach her birthplace and being killed in the attempt. And not Marietta, for Marietta was too young. Léon knew instinctively that she was incapable of the sort of evil attributed to the name of La Voisin. But if the girl and her grandmother *had* lived so near the rue Beauregard, it would explain her free use of the names of the King's mistresses, and perhaps a lot more.

The sun was sinking, the sky a blaze of gold streaked with silver clouds. In the distance were the steep roofs and high walls of a small town. To the south was Chatonnay. It was time for them to part. He had done all that could be expected of him.

He said coldly, 'That's Trélier. You'll be safe enough there. A little further is Lancerre and the sea. Here's the piece of gold I promised you and you can keep the horse.'

71

Marietta felt as if there were bands of steel around her heart. He was leaving her just as he had said he would. She would no longer have to put up with his amusement and contempt, but she felt no relief at the thought – only an overwhelming desolation.

'I don't want your gold,' she answered stiffly.

He shrugged and pocketed it. The horses pawed the ground impatiently as their riders remained motionless, the minutes lengthening as neither made any move to go off in their different directions.

Marietta cleared her throat. 'How far is it to Chatonnay?' she asked with forced carelessness.

'Three miles.' Léon knew he should be on his way. Twenty minutes and she would be safe within Trélier's walls. He was mad to think she could be in any further danger.

Marietta kept her face firmly averted from his. 'I'm a very skilled lacemaker,' she said, only her trembling hands belying her apparent calm. 'If Chatonnay has no lacemakers I would be very useful.'

'God's grace,' Léon said vehemently. 'I can't take you to Chatonnay with me!'

'Why not?' She swung round to face him.

'Because I've been away six years. What would people say if I returned home with you at my side?'

'You could tell them how you rescued me.'

72

'And have them talk even more? One hint of witchcraft and the village would be in uproar.'

'Then I'll never speak of it.'

'No. It would cause gossip that would be hurtful to Elise.'

Marietta had no need to ask if Elise was the girl he was to marry. Not only his face but his voice had softened as he said her name.

'Now God-speed before night falls,' and to her dismay he raised a hand in farewell and spurred Saracen down the darkening track.

She remained motionless, staring after him, wondering what sort of woman Elise was that she could hold the love of a man like Léon de Villeneuve for over six years. Years when countless women must have fallen under the spell of his dark eyes and sensuous mouth. At least *she* had never done so! Apart from that one brief moment when he had kissed her, she had never allowed herself to succumb to his advances.

It was cold comfort, especially as she remembered all too clearly how he had sprung away from her as if she were a leper when he had awoken to find himself in her arms. Easy to pride herself on retaining her virtue when it had never seriously been in danger.

In the distance Trélier's walls looked distinctly inhospitable. Sudden tears sprang to her eyes and she blinked them away angrily. Let his precious Elise have him. She did not want him.

A hundred yards down the track Léon reined in and looked behind him. She hadn't moved. She sat her horse, every line of her body showing tiredness and dejection. The night air was cold, and even wrapped in his cloak Léon shivered. Marietta would be half frozen before she reached Trélier and then where would she sleep? Cursing volubly, he turned Saracen round and began to ride back towards her.

Marietta heard the approaching hooves and glanced over her shoulder, fearful of a black-robed Inquisitor or sinister nobleman. Léon's face was exasperated as he rode up to her, saying curtly: 'You'll be safer at Chatonnay than in Trélier,' and then, ungraciously; 'Thank God it's dark and no one will see you!'

If she had had a shred of pride she would have told him to be on his way, but it was hard to have pride when the night was cold and dark and full of threatening shadows. He wheeled his horse around, setting off towards Chatonnay and Marietta subdued the Riccardi pride and followed.

She knew that he was furiously angry, both with himself and with her, and she despised herself for her weakness. She should have refused his offer of shelter with

74

the contempt with which it had been offered. But alone on the darkened hilltop she had felt a terror ages old, the terror of an animal being relentlessly hunted. Better the protection of a man who found her an annoyance than no protection at all. And, a small voice whispered unbidden, better still to be able to see him than never to see him again.

The sandy track curved downwards and in the moonlight Marietta could see the dark shapes of cottages and the spire of a church. It was hard to be sure but Marietta thought that Léon's shoulders looked less tense as they rode headlong down a deeply rutted lane past the church and on through the sleeping village. Her legs chafed and her back ached, and still Léon did not stop. Surely, she thought exhaustedly, surely his home could not be much further?

Léon suddenly stood up in his stirrups, giving a whoop of joy that startled Marietta so much she nearly lost her balance. Ahead of them a lantern gleamed and there came an answering shout of greeting. In the flickering light she saw an old man with a jovial face, running to greet Léon.

'Welcome home, my boy! Welcome home! I've been waiting here these past twelve hours!'

He ruffled Léon's hair in a gesture of fond intimacy. So this was Léon's father; no

75

gentlemen of quality, a farmer at the most. Marietta liked what she saw of his face, and she liked his heart-warming welcome of his grown son.

'My mother – is she awake?'

There was a chuckle. 'Aye, ever since we heard the news. Your cousin Céleste is here too, all of a twitter at your returning from court.'

For the first time the man became aware of Marietta sitting quietly on her horse, and his mouth dropped open in amazement. Léon turned in the saddle, looking at her carelessly.

'Mademoiselle Riccardi. She's in temporary need of shelter.'

'She's in temporary need of clothes, you rogue!' Armand Brissac said, delighting in Léon's impudence at bringing his whore to Chatonnay with him. That would set the cat among the pigeons! He punched him hard on the shoulder.

'It's good to have you back, Léon. The place has been a morgue without you.'

Marietta seethed silently at Léon's off-hand manner of introducing her as Léon's father led the horses at a walk, the lantern bobbing in his hand. For a few minutes she thought they were entering a wood, and then realised it was an avenue of plane trees and at the end was a château lit by so many lamps that it looked like a castle in a fairytale. Corner turrets rose ethereally in the moonlight, and there was a drawbridge and a moat, pale with water-lilies.

She felt an icy knot of apprehension in the pit of her stomach. This wasn't what she had expected and she felt suddenly nervous and unsure of herself.

'Léon! It's Léon!'

A young girl with glistening dark curls and sparkling eyes rushed into his arms as the two men dismounted and entered the château. Behind her two serving maids nudged each other and giggled as Léon swung the satin-clad figure round in his arms, and then strode through the open doors and into a room rosy with firelight.

Marietta dismounted reluctantly, feeling she was leaving her only friend behind as she patted her horse's neck and followed Léon across stone flags and into the château. The serving maids stopped their giggling and stared at her, round-eyed. Marietta was aware that not only were her feet bare, but they were dirty as well. She moved a hand up to her bodice, gathering together the tattered material and striving to make herself more respectable. Damn Léon! Where was he? At any minute the master of the château would see her and demand that she leave.

Whispering excitedly together the girls hurried in the direction of a flight of stairs, no doubt to report her presence to the *châtelaine*. Through the open door that Léon and his father had disappeared into Marietta glimpsed the dull red and blue of tapestries and the gleam of silver on a wooden dresser. Above her head a chandelier shone brightly so that she could not even disguise her disreputable appearance by standing in the shadows. She could hear a feminine voice welcoming Léon, soft and full of love. His mother, or was Elise here too?

Panic engulfed Marietta. Any minute now she would be a laughing stock. Léon had no right to bring her to such a fine place without warning her first. If his father worked for a Duc, the least he could have done was told her so, or to have lent her his cloak again. A young man in a leather jerkin and with unkempt hair stepped into the entrance hall and leered at her appreciatively. Marietta had stood enough. Léon had forsaken her: she was a fool to have come where she was not wanted.

With a pain in her chest like a knife, she ran out into the darkness. Stable boys had taken Saracen away, and ahead of her the avenue of trees rustled and soughed in the night air. Summoning all her courage, Marietta raced across the drawbridge and plunged into the terrifying blackness. She could hear shouts behind her; the sound of a man's voice calling for her to stop. She was overcome by exhaustion. She was back again in the forests of Evray, running for her life from the maddened witch-hunters. Her heart pounded, the trees cast grotesque shapes across her path, making her veer and stumble.

'Marietta! Marietta!'

The sound dinned in her ears. Marietta! Marietta Riccardi! Witch! *Witch!*

He was behind her now, only inches away. Once again she saw the flames leaping against the night sky, and then his hand caught hold of her and at his touch she screamed in fear, collapsing in a senseless heap at his feet.

Léon picked her up and carried her back into the light and warmth of the château.

'Poor girl,' his mother said as he strode with her through the room and towards the stairs. 'She must have been frightened out of her wits to run away like that.'

'She screamed just like Jacques' rabbit did when a fox got him,' Céleste said, eyeing the unconscious Marietta curiously.

'She's no rabbit,' Léon said curtly. 'She's braver than you'll ever be,' and as Céleste gasped at the uncalled-for rebuke, he carried Marietta upstairs.

'Run for Mathilde,' his mother said to Céleste. 'Léon will be undressing the girl and putting her in her shift himself!'

79

Armand Brissac grinned to himself from the doorway: his mistress disapproved of her son's womanising reputation. For Léon's sake he hoped that Mathilde was slow at obeying the order. Undressing that red-haired chit would be an enviable task. Grinning broadly to himself, he went back to the stables and the horses.

Léon laid Marietta on the huge four-poster bed and looked down at her in concern. She showed no sign of returning to consciousness. He poured water from a pitcher at the bedside, and holding her head gently tipped the glass against her lips.

His mother entered the bedchamber with Mathilde, her eyes widening. Tenderness was not a virtue she associated with her roistering son, but there was no other word to describe the expression on his face as he looked down at the dishevelled girl in his arms.

Reluctantly Léon left Marietta's side as Mathilde took over, his mother waiting pointedly until Léon had gone before allowing Mathilde to remove the mud-spattered rags that served as Marietta's clothes. She had no doubt that it was a task Léon could have accomplished expertly himself, but he was at Chatonnay now, not in the debauched court of the King.

Marietta's eyes flickered dazedly open as her gown was removed and a clean nightdress slipped over her head and shoulders. She protested weakly and a soothing voice said:

'There, my dear. There's nothing to worry about. Have a sip of verbena tea and then a long sleep, and you'll be bright as a lark in the morning.'

Marietta doubted it. Her head was spinning and every muscle in her body ached. The lady speaking so kindly to her wore a dress of soft wool, the long sleeves cuffed with fine lace. Chantilly lace, Marietta thought as she sank back against the soft pillows and closed her eyes. And hadn't she seen that face before? Only the expression in the amber eyes hadn't been one of kindness, but of mocking contempt.

'She's asleep,' Mathilde said unnecessarily.

Jeannette de Villeneuve set the verbena tea to one side and gazed down at Marietta much as her son had done earlier. 'She's a pretty girl,' she said reflectively. 'I wonder who she is?'

'No doubt we'll know soon enough,' Mathilde said, picking up Marietta's dress in her big peasant hands. 'The only place for these is the fire.' She laughed. 'Saints alive, what a pair they must have looked! A good job their road didn't take them past Lancerre.'

A faint frown creased Jeannette de Ville-neuve's brow, not at Mathilde's freedom of speech but at the thought of her future daughter-in-law. She chased it away. Léon was strong-willed and headstrong but he had always shown sound judgment. She should be grateful enough he was finally marrying, and not finding fault with his bride-to-be! If Elise Sainte-Beuve was Léon's choice then she, Jeannette, would do all she could to make her welcome at Chatonnay.

If the young lady in question wanted to be made welcome at Chatonnay. Jeannette had heard otherwise, but rumours in a small village were always rife and not to be trusted. She should have more sense than to listen to them. Already the servants' quarters would be agog at the news that Léon had returned with a barefoot and exhausted girl as companion. As to her running from the château and Léon chasing after her like a man demented, no doubt it would be spoken of for leagues around that the Lion had returned with a captive wench. A smile curved her lips as she returned to the drawing-room. Whatever the rumours, they would soon reach Lancerre, and Léon would have a hard task soothing the ruffled feathers of the beautiful widow Sainte-Beauve.

'Who is she?' she asked her son when they were finally left alone and Céleste, quickly recovering from her hurt at Léon's words, had tired of stories of Versailles and gone to bed.

Léon had already decided that in Marietta's interests the truth about her flight from Evray was best kept secret. But not where his mother was concerned. He stretched his long legs out to the roar of flaming logs, a flagon of wine in his hand, his eyes dark as he stared into the flames.

'Her name is Marietta Riccardi, and she's a lacemaker.'

His mother remained quiet, stitching at her embroidery, waiting for him to continue.

'I found her in Evray. The fools there thought she was a witch and were hunting her down to burn.'

His mother gave a gasp of horror, her embroidery falling to her lap.

'And that's not all,' Léon said, his face an impassive mask. 'They had already burned her grandmother by the time I found her.'

'Blessed Jesu,' Jeannette whispered, crossing herself. 'No wonder the poor girl was senseless with fear and exhaustion.'

'Don't you want to know if the old woman *was* a witch?' he asked curiously.

'No, I need to know nothing other than that she needs rest and sanctuary.'

'It's only fair to tell you that the old woman *did* have an uncommon knowledge of herbs and medicines,' he said, rising to his feet.

'So does Mathilde, and she's not a witch.'

Léon wondered whether to mention that Marietta's grandmother had believed herself able to protect people from poison and that it was this belief that had finally led to her death, and to the persistent hunting of Marietta. He decided against it. It was best never referred to. His hand rested lightly on her shoulder. 'What I have told you is between you and me. I want no hysterical reports of witchcraft in Chatonnay.'

'No.' Jeannette rose to her feet. 'I'm going to bed now. I'm not as young as I used to be and I tire quickly,' and then, as she reached the foot of the stairs. 'It's nice to have you home, Léon.'

He stood in front of the fire, legs apart as he watched her climb the stairs to the gallery. In his first rush of pleasure at being home he hadn't noticed how much she had changed. Her mouth was still as soft and gently smiling as when he had been a boy, but her skin had taken on a translucent texture, the once thick auburn hair was streaked with white, and he noticed that the effort of climbing the stairs made her breathe heavily, and that instead of running up them like a young girl as she had done when he was last home, she moved slowly as if with great effort.

The sooner Elise and he were married the better, he thought. Elise would be able to take the burdens off his mother's shoulders.

Only hours now until they were together and already she would have his ring on her hand. He had sent it with the fastest messenger he could find while he had waited in a fever of impatience for Louis' permission to leave court.

A log tumbled on to the hearth and Léon pushed it back with the toe of his boot. There would be no nonsense about waiting for a suitable period of mourning before he married her. The debauched mayor of Lancerre deserved no mourning. They would be married before the week was out. He drank the flagon of wine and made his way to bed, enjoying its softness after two nights spent on the road. His mother had slipped a small sachet of lavender between his sheets to scent them. Léon had to throw it savagely from the window before he could banish the unfaithful vision of Marietta next to him in the vast bed and think instead of his bride-to-be.

When Marietta awoke she was in a strange room in a comfortable four-poster bed, and wearing a nightdress that she had never seen before. She jumped from the bed in alarm and ran to the window. The vast avenue of trees that had haunted her dreams stretched out before her. She pressed a hand to her temples as memory flooded back. Léon's father was a gatekeeper or servant at a château and it was here that Léon had brought her. She glanced around the room in panic, seeing the canopied bed and ivory brushes and combs on the dressing table. What was she doing here, and who had removed her gown? Her cheeks burned as she thought of the obvious answer.

There was a light knock at the door and the satin-clad girl who had rushed into Léon's arms entered.

'I'm Céleste,' she announced simply. 'I've brought you a cup of chocolate – Aunt Jeannette said you didn't drink the verbena tea last night, and I'm not surprised. It's horrible stuff! Chocolate is much nicer. I've brought you two of my gowns as well. I couldn't bring any more because I haven't got many with me, I'm only here on a visit. But I brought my lawn green gown with the black velvet bodice and a lace-trimmed petticoat.' She spread her offerings on the bed. 'There's my best pink satin as well.' A lavish gown with a *décolletée* bodice laced with ribbon followed the lawn green rather reluctantly.

'The green one will do beautifully,' Marietta said, and was rewarded by an imperceptible sigh of relief from her benefactress.

'Would you let me do your hair?' she asked. 'I've never seen hair that colour before. Aunt Jeannette said it reminded her

86

of the setting sun.'

Marietta gathered that she had been the subject of much conversation between Céleste and her aunt as the girl continued to chatter while she dressed.

The green gown and black velvet bodice fitted to perfection, the skirt looped up to show the lace petticoat underneath. It was the finest gown Marietta had worn for many years. Seeing her reflection, and how the green flattered her colouring and the bodice showed off her figure, Marietta began to regain her confidence. It was shaken abruptly when Céleste said admiringly:

'Won't the Comte have a surprise when he sees how grand you look?'

'The Comte?' Marietta asked in alarm.

'He's waiting for you downstairs. He told me to tell you to hurry because he's expecting the widow Sainte-Beauve at any minute, but I forgot in the excitement of dressing your hair...'

While Marietta tried to gather her scattered wits Céleste grabbed her hand and hurried her from the room. Where, Marietta thought desperately, was Léon? How could he be so heartless as to leave her alone to explain her uninvited presence to this Comte?

Céleste's slippered feet ran hastily along the gallery and down the stairs and Marietta caught a glimpse of a black-wigged figure standing broad-shouldered and straight-backed beneath them, facing the fire.

She took a deep steadying breath as she reached the bottom of the stairs and began the long walk, Céleste's hand no longer in hers, across the acres of floor towards the imposing figure at the fireplace. She was vaguely aware of a woman sitting at the casement window but of no one else. There was no sign of Léon. She was going to have to face the Comte's wrath alone.

Three feet behind him she stopped and cleared her throat. 'I believe you wanted to see me, Monsieur le Comte.'

He turned, his mouth twitching with amusement.

For a moment Marietta was dumb-founded, then she felt weak with relief.

'Léon! Oh Léon, I thought you were the Comte! Has he asked to see you too? Will you explain to him?'

'There's no need to explain anything, Marietta.'

'But there is!' At the expression on his face she faltered. He took her hand gently.

'*I* am the Comte.'

She stared at him. He stood in the centre of the ornately filled room with the unmistakable stance of one who was master. He looked devastatingly handsome in a fashionable tunic of crimson velvet edged with silver braid. The black wig was his own hair, the glossy curls falling over a collar of fine *point de France* lace.

Her relief turned to anger. 'Then you could have told me earlier!'

'I didn't find the need,' Léon said easily. 'Did you sleep well?'

'Yes,' she snapped, the colour still high in her cheeks.

His face did not betray it but she knew he was laughing at her. Damnable man! There were times when she wished he had left her to her fate in the forest of Evray.

'I see that Céleste's gown fits you perfectly.' Dark eyes swept approvingly over her from head to foot.

Marietta was just about to make a sharp retort when she heard the clattering of hooves and the rattle of an approaching carriage, and Léon strode swiftly away from her as if she no longer existed.

'Our visitor,' the lady at the window said. She had been watching the heated exchange between Marietta and her son with interest. 'We will makc friends when she has gone. Céleste, perhaps you could take Marietta for something to eat while I greet Madame Sainte-Beuve?'

Disappointedly Céleste led Marietta away, not to summon a servant from the kitchen as her aunt had indicated, but upstairs to the gallery. From there she would be able to see the reunion clearly.

As Léon entered with his guest Marietta caught her breath. The word widow had not prepared her for a fragile vision in turquoise watered silk. Her face was a perfect oval, the skin flawless and as creamy as a magnolia petal, violet-blue eyes slumbrous beneath heavy, gold-tipped lashes. She was petite, the pale blonde hair that hung in clusters of ringlets scarcely skimming Léon's shoulders. A slim white hand rested securely on Léon's arms, and he was looking down at her with an expression Marietta had never been privileged to see.

'Who is she?' she asked, dreading to hear the answer.

'Elise. The widow Sainte-Beuve. The woman Léon is to marry.'

The blood drained from Marietta's face and to Céleste's horror she moved away so quickly that Léon's attention was caught. His eyes narrowed dangerously as he saw the fleeting green of her gown disappear behind a swiftly closing door. Then he was looking down at Elise again and smiling.

Céleste let out a sigh of relief. Incredible though it seemed, he had not noticed her at all.

Chapter Four

Any doubts Marietta might have had about her feelings for Léon were resolved in that one bitter moment when he looked down at the angelic face of Elise Sante-Beuve. He would never look at her like that, with a mixture of love and protectiveness and adoration. She felt a pain so intense that she had to grasp the solid wood of the bed-post for support.

There was no place for her at Chatonnay. Léon had been right in not wanting her to come. To have to endure seeing him with Elise would be a torment too unbearable to consider. Her mind made up, she felt calmer. She would leave the château and continue her journey to Venice.

The sound of movement floated upward from beneath her window. She crossed to it, seeing Léon help Elise into her carriage and then, as a coachman cracked a whip and the team of ebony-black horses began to move down the avenue of plane trees, watched unseen as Léon swung easily into Saracen's saddle, the plumes of his hat waving gently in the light breeze as he cantered beside his lady-love and out of sight.

Desolately Marietta turned away. Now was the time to go. But she couldn't take Céleste's precious green lawn with her – perhaps her aunt would give her something older and more serviceable, something the maid had no further use for. She fingered the fine material sadly. It would be hard to part with it.

'Why on earth did you move away like that?' Céleste asked, bursting into the room. 'Léon looked absolutely *furious* at being spied on.'

'I wasn't spying on him,' Marietta protested indignantly. 'It was you who wanted to watch. I didn't understand until it was too late.'

'Well, when you did understand you should have had the sense to remain quiet. Léon is quite capable of giving me a beating, even though I *am* sixteen!'

Marietta had no intention of letting Céleste know that she had already experienced that aspect of Léon's character at first hand.

Instead she said: 'I'm leaving, Céleste. I want to see your aunt and ask her if there are any old clothes she can let me have, then I'll give you your gown back. It was very kind of you to lend it.' She walked purposefully out of the room and Céleste followed her.

'Going? Going where?'

'To Venice.'

'But you can't, not without Cousin Léon's permission.'

'I can do what I want. I don't have to ask your cousin's permission for anything.'

Céleste shook her head. She liked Marietta, but her new-found friend had some strange ideas.

'Cousin Léon is the *Comte*,' she said breathlessly as she hurried after Marietta down the polished stairs. '*Everyone* has to ask his permission for everything when he is at home.'

'*I* don't,' Marietta said, and seeing Céleste's aunt, went directly to her saying simply:

'Thank you for your kindness and hospitality, madame, but I must be leaving. If there are any old clothes you could let me have so that I can return Céleste's gown, I would be most grateful.'

Jeannette looked thoughtfully at the straight-backed figure before her. Her words were calm enough, but there was a suspicious glitter of unshed tears in her eyes.

'I'm sure I can find you some more clothes, my dear. I'm sorry we had to burn the ones you arrived in, but they weren't fit to be worn again.'

Marietta's cheeks reddened in shame and Jeannette turned to Céleste.

'Would you tell Mathilde that Léon will

93

not be in for most of today? He has gone to Lancerre.'

Reluctantly Céleste left on her errand. Really it was too bad, she thought. Whenever things were beginning to get interesting she was sent out of the way!

Jeannette led Marietta out into the brilliant sunshine, saying when they could not be overheard: 'There's no need to feel uncomfortable because of the state of your clothes when you arrived. My son told me what happened to you, and I understand.'

Marietta drew in her breath sharply. It had not occurred to her that the serene-faced lady who had treated her with such kindness was Léon's mother.

Jeannette led the way through a tangle of wild flowers to a garden seat half submerged in trailing ivy. She sat down weakly, and at the sight of Jeannette's pale face Marietta immediately forgot her own troubles.

'Are you ill? Can I help you?'

Jeannette shook her head, motioning Marietta to sit beside her while she rallied her strength.

'The slightest exertion leaves me as weak as a new-born babe,' she said after a few minutes, 'but there was nowhere in the château we could talk and not be overheard, and Léon was insistent that there should be no rumours regarding the circumstances in which he found you. The peasants of

Chatonnay are as gullible as those anywhere else, I'm afraid.'

'That is one of the reasons I want to leave. Léon ... your son ... the *Comte*,' Marietta floundered. After all they had been through together it seemed perfectly natural to her to use his Christian name, but that had been before she had known his station in life. When he had been a bloodied young man who laughed easily and angered easily; now he was an elegant stranger.

Jeannette patted her hand.

'Léon is a perfectly acceptable form of address for you to use, at least when you are talking about him to me. And if you are leaving because you are frightened of the rumours that may start if you stay, then put such nonsense out of your head.'

'No, madame. It isn't only that.'

A butterfly fluttered past on azure wings and against the cloudless sky the white stone towers of the château gleamed brilliantly in the hot sun.

'Then what is it? There is no need for you to leave Chatonnay. I would like you to stay.'

Marietta, too, would have liked to stay. But not if it meant seeing Léon constantly at the side of the beautiful widow Sainte-Beuve. She bit her lip, saying so quietly that Jeannette could hardly hear her, 'There is no place for me at Chatonnay. There will be a new mistress here soon, and I doubt if she

95

would welcome my presence as you so kindly do.'

Jeannette looked at the carefully averted face, and at the nervous twisting of her fingers. So that was how the land lay. She felt a wave of compassion for the red-haired girl at her side. Léon was a notorious breaker of hearts, but so far the ladies had all been sophisticates of the court. He had no right to toy with the affections of a girl whose position was as vulnerable as Marietta's. Why, the child had no home, no family, no friends. Nothing.

'My son tells me you are a lace-maker.'

Marietta nodded, her head lifting slightly. That at least no one could take from her.

'And that you know the secret of making *point de Venise?*'

'Yes. My grandmother was a Venetian, and one of the most skilled of that city's lace-makers.'

Jeannette had found her son's careless reference as to Marietta's abilities far more interesting than he had. Indeed, she had stayed awake most of the night pondering on the possibilities that it might hold.

'I never go to court,' she continued, 'mainly because my presence is never requested, and if it were, the effort would kill me. There are so many thousands of courtiers at Versailles that most of them are hard put to it to find anywhere to lay their heads at night. But my friend, le Duc de Malbré, keeps me in touch with the latest gossip and fashions and I know that *point de Venise* lace is the rage.'

'That is because it is the finest lace in the world,' Marietta said proudly.

'And I also know that our own country's lacemakers are trying desperately hard to imitate it.'

'And failing,' Marietta said, a smile returning to her face. It was a pretty face, guileless and generous. Jeannette was liking Marietta Riccardi more and more with every passing minute. She had seen the concern in the girl's eyes when she had sunk weakly on to the seat; it had been a genuine concern. Marietta Riccardi would make a good friend. And a good wife.

She banished the thought as soon as it entered her head. Léon was to marry Elise and Elise was as sweet-tempered as she was sweet-looking. It was stupid of her still to entertain doubts as to whether such a fragile and helpless girl could make her swash-buckling son a suitable wife.

'I have also heard that the King's Comptroller, Colbert, is trying to prevent its importation, and that the finest names in the land smuggle it in, hiding it under their cloaks. Le Duc tells me that Colbert desperately wants to start production of *point de Venise* in France and put an end to the smuggling. He estimates that losing the lace trade to Venice is costing the country something in the region of three million *livres* a year. Your work must have been much in demand.'

'Not in Evray,' Marietta said bitterly. 'There was no one in Evray in need of lace.'

'But in Paris?'

'In Paris we were sought after by such people as Madame de Montespan herself.'

'Who no doubt wanted you to work solely for her? I doubt if Madame de Montespan would like sharing such a source of supply.'

Marietta's smile widened. 'Indeed she did not. We were hard put to it to keep up with her demands.'

Jeannette nodded thoughtfully. 'Did you ever consider teaching others to make *point de Venise*, and so enlarge your business?'

'My grandmother would have died first. She always said that the making of *point de Venise* was a Venetian art and should remain so.'

Jeannette nodded. She had suspected as much.

'I would like you to do something for me. I would like you to walk through the garden. The kitchen garden is to the right, beyond that barrier of wild roses. And then I would like you to take a careful look at the château, and when you have done that ask Armand for a horse and take a ride through the village and surrounding countryside. When you have done all that we will continue our talk.'

Marietta wondered if perhaps Madame de Villeneuve was a little wanting in the head. One glance at those intelligent dark eyes was enough to assure her that she was not.

'If that is what you want me to do, madame.'

'It is,' Jeannette said, rising to her feet. 'We'll meet again this evening. There's plenty of cold meat and fruit in the kitchen – take some with you when you go riding. I'll tell Mathilde to put wine and bread in your saddlebag as well.'

She began to walk with disturbing slowness down the overgrown path and back towards the château.

Puzzled, Marietta set off obediently towards the kitchen garden. Not until she had conquered the shoulder-high barrier of sweet-smelling roses did she realise that she had intended leaving immediately, and would now be unable to do so, at least until evening, and she did not relish the thought of setting off on her long journey in the darkness. Whether intentionally or unintentionally, Madame de Villeneuve had seen to it that she would see Léon once more before she left. Marietta did not know whether to be glad or sorry.

The kitchen garden was so overgrown that

unless Léon's mother had told her it was one, Marietta would never have guessed. A small patch had been cleared and a few herbs grew alongside beans and asparagus. Pear trees and apple trees were heavy with fruit but early windfalls lay rotting and ungathered.

Marietta frowned. Her impression the previous night had been that of entering a magnificent château. Now, in the harsh sunlight, she saw that her initial assumption of wealth had been incorrect. There was clearly no one to carry out that most vital of tasks, the tending of the vegetables, and as she approached the château she saw that there was an air of genteel poverty about it. The enormous room that had been the scene of Léon's reunion with Elise was the only room, with the exception of her own bedchamber, that looked cared for.

For the first time the suspicion entered Marietta's head that the room she had slept in had been prepared for Léon. Everywhere else there was dust and a general air of neglect. To Mathilde's indignation she opened store-cupboards and pantries: the contents were meagre. No satisfying stocks of salted and pickled preserves met her eyes, no large amounts of jam. Barely anything at all.

Mathilde was not used to having her kitchen scrutinised and gave Marietta her meat and fruit with bad grace. Marietta was hardly aware of it. She was too deep in thought. The maids who had stared at her the previous evening were half-heartedly making bread, but talking so much that Marietta doubted they would ever finish their task.

Armand grinned welcomingly at her when she found her way to the stables and asked for a horse. He had dutifully saddled Saracen earlier on and privately thought his master a fool for spending time on the fragile widow Sainte-Beuve when there was much better sport at home. His hand lingered a fraction too long on Marietta's ankle as she mounted the horse, and he was rewarded with a sharp cuff on his ear. It didn't disconcert him in the slightest. He spat gustily and watched with admiration as Marietta handled the strange horse with ease.

He doubted if the widow Sainte-Beuve had ever been astride a horse. The Riccardi wench looked as if she had been born on one. He rubbed his stinging ear and went back to his work, grinning.

She rode in a cloud of dust through the village of Chatonnay. The peasants paused in their work, watching her curiously. The horse belonged to the Comte. Who did the girl belong to? Barefoot, ragged children left the turkeys they were tending and ran after her, shouting and laughing.

Most of the fields being tended were growing woad or maize. There were vines in profusion and very little else. A pathetically thin girl, not much older than herself, grabbed a naked baby out of the way of Marietta's horse and it wailed angrily, beating tiny fists against her chest as Marietta rode by.

By the time she returned to the château she had seen all that she needed to. Chatonnay was as impoverished as any other village in France, and despite Léon's fine clothes, his home was impoverished too. No doubt it had been a long time since he had been home, and at the moment all he had eyes for was Elise. Marietta wondered if he was even aware of his mother's precarious state of health.

With relief she saw that Saracen had not returned to the stables; it would be impossible to talk to his mother in Léon's disturbing presence. She went to her bedchamber, washed her hands and face in cold water, brushed her hair which had blown into its usual wild tangle, and went in search of Madame de Villeneuve.

Jeannette was at the dining table waiting for her. She poured her a goblet of apple wine, and not until they had finished the hare pie and artichokes did she ask, 'Well, my dear, what did you think of your exploration?'

'I thought that life at Chatonnay was as difficult as life anywhere.'

'Except at court,' Jeannette agreed drily.

Marietta remained silent, wondering what it was that Léon's mother wanted of her.

'For the Villeneuves, too, times have been difficult. Now, thanks to Léon's success, we no longer have to count every *livre,* but it will take months to restore the château to anything like its former comfort; and will be of very little help to the villagers. They need to be able to earn money for themselves, not rely on the Comte's bounty, however generous.'

At last Marietta understood what it was Léon's mother wanted of her. She said slowly, 'You mean that *point de Venise* lace could bring prosperity to Chatonnay?'

'Yes.'

The two women stared at each other and Marietta's struggle showed in her eyes.

'The skill is passed down from mother to daughter. It is a jealousy guarded secret; if it was not then the whole world could make *point de Venise* and Venice would no longer be rich.'

'I know.' Jeannette's voice was understanding, and Marietta knew that if she refused she would incur no wrath, but it was hard to refuse Madame de Villeneuve anything. Beneath her wan pallor and physical weakness was an inner strength. She did not want the secret for herself or for her own gain, only for the peasants who scratched out a living on the sun-baked land and to whom her son was Comte and Seigneur.

'It would take too long, madame. Such skills cannot be learned in a few days or a few weeks. True lacemaking is not for amateurs.'

'But if you stayed...'

'No.' Marietta's voice was firm. 'I cannot stay.'

Jeannette sighed. The girl was right. It would not be fair on either her or Elise.

'All right,' she said, admitting defeat. 'But one thing I do insist upon. You can't leave here until you have something of worth to sell on your journey. Stay here and make some collars and cuffs, then at least you will have enough to reach Narbonne or Trélier. And take my advice, Marietta. Settle there. To attempt the journey across the Alps to Venice would be madness, and you will not easily find a ship to take you by sea.'

Marietta did not agree but was too polite to argue and Jeannette's suggestion that she make some collars and cuffs before setting out on the road was a sensible one. Yet Léon would be here...

Jeannette began to cough, a harsh racking cough that brought Marietta from her seat and round the table to her. When at last Jeannette leaned back in her chair, the handkerchief she had clutched to her mouth was bright with spots of blood.

'Don't tell Léon,' she said, seeing the expression on Marietta's face. 'There is the wedding to prepare for before I can allow myself the luxury of being ill and taking to my bed.'

'But you can't prepare for a wedding!' Marietta said, horrified. 'You've scarcely the strength to walk up the stairs!'

'I must.' Jeannette's face was tortured.

Marietta thought of Mathilde and the two carefree serving maids. Apart from them and Armand and the stable boy, there was no one to help Jeannette with the preparations. She took Jeannette de Villeneuve's hand, knowing that she could not let the sick woman who had taken her in and given her shelter cope with the wedding preparations single-handed.

'Let me help,' she said. 'I'm a good cook, and I can do all the baking that is necessary.'

Jeannette's look of gratitude was all the thanks she needed. The older woman squeezed her hand tight.

'Just one more favour, Marietta. Don't tell Léon how ill I am. There will be plenty of time for that after the wedding.'

Before Marietta could protest there came the sound of Léon's familiar stride and within seconds he was in the room, drawing his gauntlets and throwing them on to a convenient chair, doffing his plumed hat of ostrich feathers and setting it carelessly down beside the gloves.

Mathilde hurried in with more hare pie and Marietta sat down again, such a tight constriction round her chest that she wondered if she, too, was sickening for something.

'How is Elise?' Jeannette asked.

Her son frowned, broke his wheaten bread in half and said: 'She seems to think we should postpone the wedding out of respect to Sainte-Beuve.'

'Well, he *has* only just died. She should still be in mourning.'

'For that old lecher?' Léon asked savagely.

Jeannette seemed to be choosing her words with great care.

'Elise did seem to adapt very well to living with an older man.'

Léon's black brows drew together till they almost met. 'She hadn't much choice had she? Forced into marriage at seventeen with a man already a grandfather. God, even to think about it...'

'But she never seemed really unhappy, Léon.'

'Of course she was unhappy!' her son retorted angrily.

Jeannette bit her lip, knowing that Léon was on the verge of losing his temper. 'He took very great care of her,' she persisted.

106

The retort that sprang to Léon's lips was quickly suppressed. He was speaking to his mother, not a soldier, and for the first time he became aware of Marietta's presence.

'You don't understand. I don't give a damn for the niceties. Elise has had a life of hell for six years, and there's no need for a period of mourning. And I won't have her married from his house! I'll marry her here!'

He pushed his plate of hare pie away unfinished, glared at Marietta as if the whole exchange had been her fault and strode away from the room. Jeannette sighed and shook her head weakly.

'I've tried to tell him before but he won't listen. Elise was *happy* with old Sainte-Beuve. He looked after her as if she were a child, treating her like a piece of precious china, but Léon's pride won't let him admit it. I daresay he's left Elise in tears by his stubborn insistence on going ahead with the wedding without waiting for a suitable period of mourning.'

She raised a hand to her throbbing temples. 'We must make a start on the pies and the cakes tomorrow and where I shall get the strength from I don't know. And there are all the rooms to prepare. Elise couldn't possibly manage with just Mathilde to look after her. She has an army of servants at Lancerre. She'll have to bring them with her and they'll have to have room to sleep and most of the rooms haven't been opened since my husband died. I've kept asking Mathilde to make a start on them but she can't get any obedience out of those girls and her days are busy enough as it is…'

'Please don't worry,' Marietta said, trying not to let her hurt show at the way Léon had glared at her and the protective way he spoke about Madame Sainte-Beuve. 'I'll look after everything for you.'

Jeannette undid the ring of keys at her waist. 'Then please do, Marietta. Though it will need a miracle to prepare for the wedding *and* put the château in order.'

'Not a miracle,' Marietta said, forcing a smile, 'just hard work. I think you should rest now. Would you like me to help you up the stairs?'

Gratefully, Jeannette took her arm. Léon, still incensed at his mother's insinuations, stormed out of his room intent on continuing the conversation. It was an insult to Elise to suggest that she had been even remotely happy in her marriage to the Mayor of Lancerre.

He was stopped short by the sight of Marietta half carrying his mother up the stairs. His anger vanished in an instant. Appalled, he took the steps two at a time, lifting his mother in his arms and carrying her the rest of the way to her bed. The door closed behind mother and son and Marietta went to her own room and slowly removed Céleste's green gown and slipped into her nightdress.

If Elise had been happy in her marriage to her elderly husband, how much happier would she be as Léon's bride? And for the sake of Jeannette, Marietta would have to be a witness to that happiness. The night was warm, but Marietta felt chilled to the bone as she lay in the darkness. He had not even spoken a word to her tonight. As far as Léon de Villeneuve was concerned, she no longer existed. The night sky was already paling to dawn before she finally closed her eyes and fell into a restless sleep.

Marietta was wrong in thinking Léon oblivious of the shabbiness that his home had fallen into. Or that he was unaware of Jeannette's failing health. His reunion with Elise had not been all he had anticipated, and he had ridden away from Lancerre in a mood of irritation. Elise's reluctance for an early marriage had been the main cause of it. He had taken it for granted that her love for him would overrule the outward proprieties, yet her violet-blue eyes had been distressed when he had told her of his intention for an early marriage, and she had stiffened awkwardly in his arms, feeling it wrong for him to kiss her with her husband barely cold in his grave.

As far as Léon was concerned it was all damned annoying, and for some reason he couldn't define, his irritation had deepened when he had walked into the dining-room and seen Marietta and his mother in close conversation. The green lawn dress was modest enough on Céleste; on Marietta it took on a whole new meaning. High rounded breasts peeped tantalisingly from the black velvet bodice and the soft falls of the skirt accentuated the pleasing outline of her hips.

His feelings were mixed when Jeannette had told him that she had asked Marietta to stay and help her prepare for the wedding. He was honourable enough to feel a measure of relief that she wouldn't be leaving Chatonnay without means of support. His mother's idea that she employed herself making collars and cuffs in *point de Venise* was a sensible one. The smallest amount of such lace would fetch a high price. Yet she brought out in him feelings that were not fitting in a man approaching marriage. He remembered the tantalising smallness of her waist and the way her hair had glinted a thousand shades of red in the candlelight, hanging down to her waist in gleaming waves and curls without even a ribbon to restrain them. No wonder the Huguenots said a woman's hair was the work of the Devil. Marietta could tempt even a saint from the path of virtue, and Léon de Villeneuve had never aspired to sainthood.

'I need her,' Jeannette had said simply and Léon, looking down at her, knew that it was true and that he was glad of it. He groaned inwardly. The sooner he was married the better. Celibacy was no way of life for a man who had spent six years at the court of Louis XIV.

Despite her lack of sleep Marietta rose early. The clink of the keys at her waist gave her confidence. She had two weeks to effect a transformation at Chatonnay; there was no time to lose lying abed. Mathilde and the serving maids were outraged at having their presence demanded in the kitchen at such an early hour, and it was Marietta who cooked Léon's breakfast, though she handed it to Mathilde to carry through to the dining table.

Léon sat down to it with relish. Mathilde's breakfasts were usually notoriously slipshod.

'You've surpassed yourself this morning, Mathilde,' he said, giving her a smile that made even old Mathilde wish she were a young girl again.

'Wasn't me,' she admitted reluctantly. 'Seems we've got a new *châtelaine* here, though Heaven alone knows why. Forty

111

years I've been here and never a word of complaint, and now a slip of a girl is given Madame's keys and is ordering us about left, right and centre. She'd cooked a whole batch of bread before I got down this morning, as if the bread Lili and Cécile made yesterday was not good enough.'

She left the room muttering angrily beneath her breath. Léon was unable to sympathise. He had never tasted such good bread; Marietta obviously had talents other than lacemaking. He had no time to waste in telling her so, however. Elise was waiting and so was the *Abbé*. There was a wedding to arrange and he still had to coax Elise into agreeing to it at the earliest opportunity.

By the time he strode across to the stables and a waiting and saddled Saracen, Marietta had already sent an eager Lili down into the village to request the help of her sisters, and had cleared the whole contents of the kitchen into the yard, sweeping every inch of the stone flags with a broom. The dust rose in choking clouds, sending Mathilde scurrying for cover.

'Whenever I see you,' Léon said, a wide grin on his face as he paused at the doorway, 'you always have a dirty face!'

'And you always have bad manners!' Marietta returned, wielding the broom with gusto so that a cloud of dust threatened to spoil the perfection of his dove-grey tunic and white leather boots. He retreated hastily and Marietta continued her sweeping with angry force. His precious Elise would look like a goose-girl too if she had such a kitchen to contend with! She looked so fierce as she ordered Cécile to begin sluicing the flags with scalding hot water that Cécile did not dare demur. By midday scoured pans gleamed, the giant wood table was near white and the flags were not only washed but white-stoned. A large jug of flowers stood on the window-sill.

Lili's two sisters were only too happy to work and Marietta sent them to the upstairs room, beating carpets, airing beds, scrubbing floors. Linen-cupboards were turned out and Mathilde was set the task of darning and patching. The chicken that Marietta put in the pot, aided by a bunch of herbs growing wild in the garden, tasted more appetising than anything else before served on the de Villeneuves' dining table.

By the end of the week even Mathilde had been won over, and with the help of Lili and her sisters the château was spotlessly clean, the rooms for Elise and her maids prepared, and the fragrance of fresh flowers mingled with that of new-baked bread and the enticing odours of a perpetual stockpot. She had gone to Armand next for help, explaining that she needed the kitchen garden cleared and the fruit gathered in. An

113

hour later an army of ragamuffins between five and ten years old descended on the wilderness of the garden, and under Marietta's direction began to clear it. Cécile, once shown how, proved an excellent jam-maker and under the blazing southern sun Marietta laboured happily in the garden, rescuing what she could of the herbs, bringing about some semblance of order.

'But what about your lacemaking?' Jeannette had protested as Marietta sat sewing new curtains for Elise's bed-chamber.

'Tomorrow,' Marietta said, and then without looking up from her work, 'Cécile is going to watch me. She should be an apt pupil. She's quick and intelligent and clever with her fingers.'

Jeannette looked over at the Titian-haired head bending low over her needlework, knowing what an enormous gesture it was for her to show anyone but another Venetian the secrets of her craft.

'Change your mind and stay, Marietta. I shall miss you dreadfully when you leave.'

'No. Elise will be here to keep you company.' She pricked her finger on the needle and blamed that for the sudden rush of tears to her eyes. What was she doing sewing bed-curtains for Elise's bridal chamber?

She blinked the tears away. She was sewing curtains to help Jeannette. She must not dwell on the use to which they would be put, but hard as she tried she could not help it. With her own hands she was labouring to make the new bride's bedchamber as pleasant and comfortable as possible. The room faced south, full of brilliant sun and the sound of birds. It was there that Léon and Elise would lie together, there that their children would be born.

There came the sound of a door slamming and Léon's footsteps across the hall. Hastily Marietta picked up her work.

'I'm tired. Goodnight Jeannette,' and she hurried from Jeannette's small drawing-room only seconds before Léon entered.

Jeannette knew the reason for her speedy exit and her heart ached for her, but there was nothing she could do. Léon wanted to marry Elise. Had always wanted to marry Elise. She sighed and turned to meet him.

Chapter Five

Léon sat down on the red brocade chair that Marietta had just vacated, and was instantly aware of the disturbing fragrance of faint lavender. He stretched his long, booted legs out to the fire and frowned, his forehead deeply furrowed. Jeannette eyed him curiously. It seemed to her that for a prospective bridegroom Léon was showing disturbing signs of boredom.

He poured himself a goblet of wine, took a sip and raised his eyebrows.

'It's cinnamon-scented,' Jeannette said in answer to his unspoken question. 'Marietta made it.' Léon made no comment, but she noticed that he helped himself very quickly to more.

'Le Duc de Malbré and Raphael arrive tomorrow from Paris.'

Léon nodded, pleased. The Duke was an old friend of Jeannette's and Raphael a companion he had played and wrestled with as a child and drunk and womanised with as a man. They were the first of the wedding guests to take up residence at Chatonnay, and Chatonnay – to Léon's relief – was now fit to receive them. Despite his pleasure his brow remained furrowed as he said:

'Armand's daughter has gone down with fever.'

Jeannette's face whitened. 'Is it small-pox?'

'Armand says not, but she's eating and drinking nothing. He will need to stay with her for the next few days.'

Jeannette did not feel reassured. Two village girls had died of fever in the last three months, but there was no point in worrying Léon with such knowledge.

The wine mellowed him, and he gazed around his home well pleased. It would be good to have Raphael's company, and to-morrow night Elise was dining with them. Candlelight shone on polished wood, and a magnificent vase of flowers crowned the table. Thanks to Marietta, Chatonnay was fit to receive anyone who chose to come. Her cinnamon wine was good too, and the Duke had an appreciative palate. He poured himself another goblet full, whistled his dogs, and made his way to bed.

Marietta, on hearing of Armand's daughter's illness, had immediately visited her. The girl was raging with fever and thin to a point of emaciation. She ordered Armand to feed her goat's milk and honey, and was horrified when Armand protested that they had no such luxuries.

'Anyone can keep bees!' she told Jeannette indignantly. 'And as for goats...'

'But we *have* a goat,' Jeannette protested weakly.

'What good is one? What about the villagers? They are too poor to buy their own. What do they do for milk?'

'I'm sure that now Léon is back he will...'

'Pah,' Marietta said, her hands on her hips, her eyes flashing. 'Léon is too busy paying court to Madame Sainte-Beuve to worry his head about goats! I'll drive the cart to Montpellier and bring back a dozen of them. There are children in Chatonnay dying for lack of milk, and the least the de Villeneuves can do as Seigneur is to provide that for them!'

Weakly Jeannette agreed, handed Marietta a purse full of *livres* and wondered exactly where Marietta intended penning the animals once she had bought them.

On seeing her march purposefully across the cobbled yard to the stables the stable boy brightened up considerably and moved towards the mare, intending to saddle it. 'The cart,' Marietta said briefly, 'and both the mules.'

The stable boy stared.

'Oh for goodness' sake be quick about it,' Marietta said exasperatedly, 'or it will be noon before I leave!'

The stable boy debated whether it was

119

worth risking a thick ear by letting his hand linger on her waist on the pretext of helping her into the cart, and was cheated of the chance as she sprang on to the rough wood seat unaided and grasped the reins. He stared fascinated at well-shaped bare feet. No lady would travel thus, and yet the de Villeneuves treated her as an equal and she certainly had high ideas of herself. There was as much chance of tumbling her in the straw like Cécile or Lili as tumbling Madam de Villeneuve herself.

Intrigued, he watched as the shabby cart trundled out through the courtyard and across the drawbridge. Barefoot or not, Marietta held herself like a queen. He wondered if the Comte had enjoyed the pleasures so firmly denied himself and grinned lasciviously. There could be no other reason for her being at Chatonnay. Hell and the Devil, but he wished he'd been born a man with money! The sight of Marietta's high rounded breasts had put all thought of work out of his head.

He threw the saddle he was cleaning to one side and crept round to the kitchen door. With a bit of luck Cécile would be able to slip away from Mathilde's suspicious eyes and sneak into the back of the stables with him. She was short and dumpy, but it was dark in the stables and a man had to use his imagination. When the Comte had had his fill of the Riccardi wench she wouldn't be quite so high and mighty, and could very well be glad of his attentions.

Living in hope, he whistled softly through the open back door and was rewarded by seeing Cécile's plain face light up as she gave a quick look round to ensure no one was watching, and then hurried towards him.

Montpellier was hot and crowded, and it took Marietta the best part of the morning to haggle for the goats she wanted. The stupid animals had no desire to jump into the cart voluntarily, and only with much help and ribaldry from the local stall-holders did she manage to herd the protesting goats into the wooden cart. Even then her troubles were not over. The animals smelt abominably and nosed their way over her shoulder and beneath her arm as she urged the mules through the narrow streets and out on to the dusty road to Chatonnay.

If she'd had any sense she would have stayed with Ninette Brissac and asked Armand to bring the wretched animals himself, she thought savagely as an un-grateful animal gave her a nip on the arm.

It was past midday, and the light was clear with a luminosity that Marietta had never seen anywhere else but in Languedoc. The sun-scorched track wound through olive groves and fig trees, and Marietta raised her face to the sun and tried to ignore the reek and clamour of the goats. From behind her came the thundering of hooves and the crack of a whip and she turned her head to see an outrider and a team of beautifully matched greys with scarlet plumes drawing an impressive carriage. Hastily she urged the mules out of the way to let the splendid equipage pass.

It didn't. Instead it halted and the outrider, magnificent in black velvet with falls of lace at throat and cuff and knee-high boots of gleaming black leather reined in and said furiously, 'What the devil do you think you are doing?'

Marietta gritted her teeth, pushed an inquisitive goat away from her neck and said: 'Providing Chatonnay with goats for milk, which is something *you* should have done long ago!'

Léon's face was white with anger. 'Hell's light, aren't there men enough to ferry goats without you making a public spectacle of yourself?'

From the windows of the coach two occupants watched, one in amusement, the other in admiration. The Duke de Malbré's lips twitched at the sight of his elegant young friend being spoken to in such a way by a peasant girl. His son, Raphael, was staring with blatant admiration.

There was a smudge of dirt on her cheek, the hem of her gown was thick with dust, yet she was the most ravishing creature he had ever seen. Green eyes slanted tantalisingly upwards, bright with anger. Olive skin gleamed flawlessly, and for the first time in his life Raphael de Malbré decided that the women of Versailles were fools. Why strive with creams and lotions for a face as white as death when there was beauty such as this in nature?

Her lips were full and soft, cherry-red. Her nose was straight, her face heart-shaped, and her hair... Dear Lord! Raphael de Malbré gazed mesmerised. Never in his life had he seen hair like it. All of a sudden he was looking forward to more than a few weeks hawking and hunting with his friend. With village girls like this in Chatonnay his visit was going to be a memorable one.

'Armand is with Ninette, and who else is there?' Marietta was saying fiercely, fighting back tears of humiliation as she saw the amused expression on the exquisitely dressed occupant of the carriage and the all-too familiar look in the younger man's eyes. She might as well be naked the way he was looking at her, and as for Léon... He looked as if he could quite happily choke her to death.

'How dare you behave like a peasant!' he

hissed through clenched teeth. 'You've shamed me in front of my guests, made your position at Chatonnay impossible…'

A goat, taking advantage of the Stationary carriage, jumped nimbly beneath Marietta's arm and on to the ground.

'Now see what you've done,' Marietta cried, jumping down from the cart. 'Do you know how long it took me to get these stupid animals into the cart in the first place?' Breathlessly she raced after it, picking up her skirts to run the faster.

'Hell's light!' Léon seized his riding crop and leapt from Saracen's back, running after her.

'Do you realise what a spectacle you're making of us?' Eyes that were once honey-gold were black as the Devil's as he seized the goat's hind legs while Marietta held frantically on to the front ones. The goat squirmed, depositing a large amount of straw and stale dung on to Léon's immaculate black velvet.

'God's grace!'

She thought he was going to strike her as she hauled the goat from his grasp, and he brushed angrily at the offending dirt.

The sight of Léon, sophisticate of Versailles and warrior of the battlefield, struggling with an unkempt village girl and protesting goat was too much for the de Malbrés. The Duke was wiping his eyes with

124

a lace kerchief, while Raphael's laughter was loud enough to be heard both in Montpellier and Chatonnay at the same time.

Léon struggled to speak, failed, clenched his fists and swung on his heel, leaving Marietta to struggle with the still writhing goat as he mounted Saracen, his shoulders rigid with anger.

Raphael de Malbré, still laughing uproariously, blew her a kiss from the window of the carriage as she sat, the goat in her lap, her skirts high around her knees.

'Not even a pair of shoes on her feet!' Léon said explosively to his mother when the de Malbrés had been settled in their rooms. 'Driving the mule and cart like the commonest peasant, and with one hundred and fifty goats in the back!'

'Twelve,' his mother said, biting her lip to prevent herself from laughing.

'Twelve, twenty, one hundred, what difference does it make? How am I going to introduce her to the de Malbrés now?'

'As a kind-hearted girl willing to ride in the heat to Montpellier for goats to provide milk for the peasants who live on *our* land and cannot afford goats of their own.'

'Any of the village men could have gone for the goats.'

'And drunk the money,' Jeannette replied equably. 'You should be proud of Marietta, not ashamed. The goats and bees will make a big difference, not only to us but to all those who depend on us.'

There was a long silence and then Léon said in a voice dangerously quiet, 'What bees?'

Jeannette winced. She had meant to break the news of the bees gently, not blurt it out while Léon was still in a raging temper over the goats.

'What bees?' he repeated, eyes smouldering.

'The ones in the orchard. Marietta thought it would be a good idea to…'

The door slammed behind him and Jeannette sank down into a chair and poured herself a restorative glass of plum brandy.

Lili and Cécile scuttled out of his way as he stormed through the château and out into the orchard. What yesterday had been a wilderness was now transformed by line upon line of neatly arranged bee-hives. Close by, penned in the meadow adjacent to the kitchen garden, the goats grazed peacefully.

Léon swore, but this time in reluctant admiration. In a week she had done more for Chatonnay than Mathilde had ever done. And the sight of her in that cart surrounded by goats was not one he would forget in a hurry. He grinned, his anger disappearing as quickly as it had been aroused. The Lord alone knew what the two of them had looked like, struggling with that wretched animal! No wonder Henri and Raphael had laughed themselves senseless. If word of it reached Versailles his reputation would be ruined. He determined to threaten Raphael with a cracked jaw if he even so much as whispered about it.

'What's her name?' Raphael called from behind him and Léon turned to see his friend approach, his travelling clothes changed for a slashed doublet that showed the finery of his Dutch linen shirt and a pair of breeches tied above the knee with a profusion of ribbons in the style affected by anyone with any pretensions to fashion. It was reputed at court that Raphael de Malbré had used as much as two hundred and fifty yards of silver ribbon in one outfit. He was as tall as Léon but slimmer, his hair carefully powdered. In the orchard, the air heavy with the hum of bees and the drifting aroma of goats, he looked out of place – like an exotic bird in a farmyard of hens.

'Who?' Léon asked, knowing very well who his womanising friend meant.

'The red-haired wench with the goats. Hell and damnation, I've never seen a sight like her.' He rubbed well-manicured hands in anticipation. 'I've not had sport with a village girl for years, but I'm going to make up for it now. Did you see that hair and those breasts? They're enough to make a monk break his vows! Now, what's her name and where can I find her?'

'Her name,' Léon said with a sudden spurt of anger, 'is Marietta Riccardi, and you can find her at my dinner table,' and he turned his back on his dumbfounded friend and strode back into the kitchen.

'How was I to know Léon would be riding back on the Montpellier road with his guests?' Marietta asked Céleste bad-temperedly as she hooked her into her gown.

Céleste giggled. 'But with a cartload of goats! What *will* the Duke think?'

'I don't know and I don't care,' Marietta lied, beginning to brush her hair fiercely.

'Well, you can't wear the lawn green again, the hem is thick with dust. *My* gowns never get in such a state!'

'*You* don't buy goats.'

'I should think not!' Céleste shuddered with horror. 'Nasty, smelly things. Have you seen the gown Aunt Jeannette has laid out for you? I think the colour a little drab myself, but at least it's better than my lawn green, and I *can't* lend you my pink satin. I must look my best tonight. Raphael de Malbré is reputed to be the handsomest man in the whole of Paris, excepting Léon

128

of course, but Léon is to marry Elise so he doesn't count.'

She chattered on happily as Marietta stepped into a dress of heavy amber velvet. The colour glowed like autumn leaves, the perfect foil for her hair and eyes, and it was no accident that the deep scooped neck and nipped-in waist fitted to perfection, or that the full-blown sleeves gathered in so tightly at the wrists. Jeannette had spent all day sewing and altering and making sure that the dress that had been hers would look as if it had been made for Marietta and for no one else.

The Duke de Malbré had accepted Jeannette's explanation that Marietta was an old friend, staying with them until the wedding, with a grave face and a twinkle in his eyes. He had known the de Villeneuves for years and had never before met anyone who even remotely resembled the red-haired vixen who had given Léon such a tongue-lashing as they struggled over the goat. As for why any lady of quality should be riding around the countryside barefoot and driving a mule, Jeannette had made no attempt to explain and the Duke had the manners not to press her. It would, he thought, be rather hard for even Jeannette to think up a plausible explanation.

Raphael had been first disappointed, and then delighted. Disappointed because it meant if the girl was no local peasant there was no way he could enjoy her body without preamble; delighted because it meant he would be in her company for long periods, and with Léon on the verge of matrimony he would have no competition. Like his father, he found the de Villeneuves' explanation of Marietta's presence too vague to be satisfying, but it added piquancy to the situation. Was the girl Léon's mistress, and was he reluctant to give her up even though he was about to marry? It wouldn't be the first time he and Léon had vied for the favours of the same lady. This time he, Raphael, had a distinct advantage, for Marietta Riccardi could not be happy at the prospect of Léon marrying and so would be more than willing to find consolation in other arms, and Léon could do very little about it. For if he did, his bride-to-be would discover his secret. Raphael had lost too many ladies to Léon's dark charms not to feel a certain sense of satisfaction. Marietta Riccardi did not know it, but in Raphael de Malbré's eyes she was his already.

With throbbing nerves Marietta followed Céleste along the gallery and down the broad sweep of the stairs. Léon was leaning against the fireplace, a wine glass in his hand. Unlike his friend, his hair was still unpowdered, hanging in glossy curls over the exquisite lace of his falling collar. He was dressed in scarlet velvet, the well-shaped legs adorned with garter ruffs and the heels of his buckled shoes fashionably high.

Marietta took a deep trembling breath and steeled herself to meet his gaze. She felt her legs weaken with shock as instead of the blazing anger she expected she saw at first startled surprise and then open admiration.

The low neckline of her dress was laced with silk ribbon, the bodice embroidered with tiny mother-of-pearl flowers. A string of Jeannette's pearls circled the base of her throat and the fiery cloud of her hair had been swept by Céleste into glistening ringlets in the manner of a lady of fashion.

He felt his throat constrict. Lord of Grace, even with Elise at his side she set his blood on fire. He mastered his emotions, turning graciously to the delicate figure of his bride-to-be as he introduced the two girls.

The moment Marietta had dreaded had arrived. Elise Sainte-Beuve looked like a china doll in a gown of ice-blue grosgrain silk, corn-coloured ringlets falling to her naked shoulders. She took Marietta's hand and gave her a smile of incredible sweetness. If Lancerre and Chatonnay were rife with rumours of the red-haired wench the Lion of Languedoc had returned with, they had not reached Madame Sainte-Beuve. There

was no hint of jealousy in her eyes, no dis-
approval.

'I've been looking forward to meeting
you,' she said, her voice so soft it was
scarcely more than a whisper. 'I've asked
Léon to bring you with him when he visits
me. There are not many people of my own
age to be friends with in Lancerre.'

Marietta stared at her helplessly. She had
hated this woman who had Léon's love and
now, face to face with her, the hatred she
had nursed was evaporating as fast as dew
on a summer morning.

'Le Duc de Malbré,' Leon said and
Marietta found her hand being kissed by the
distinguished gentleman who had watched
her with such amusement earlier in the day.
He was in his early fifties and wore shoes
that were high heeled and studded with tiny
diamonds. His suit was of dark blue velvet,
the collars and cuffs embellished with gold
lace. *Point de Venise* lace. She suppressed a
smile, wondering if the elegant Duke was
one of those who smuggled the precious
commodity into the country under cover of
his cloak.

'And Raphael de Malbré,' Léon's voice
changed slightly as his dashing friend took
Marietta's hand and kissed it for far longer
than was necessary.

'My pleasure, mademoiselle. If I had
known Chatonnay held such treasures I

would have journeyed here long ago.'

'And would have been disappointed,' Léon said, trying to keep a note of irritation out of his voice. 'Mademoiselle Riccardi is staying here only for a brief period. Her home is in Venice.'

'Her home,' Raphael de Malbré said, blue eyes alight with undisguised admiration, 'should be Versailles. Her beauty far exceeds that of the famed ladies of the court.'

Léon firmly took Raphael's arm and led his friend to where Céleste waited in a fever of impatience to be introduced. Her jealousy at the flattery he had bestowed upon Marietta was soothed by his fulsome compliments as to her own beauty. But the fire in his eyes that Marietta had kindled was no longer there as he kissed Céleste's plump little hand, and Léon's sharp eyes were well aware of it. He would have to inform Raphael in no uncertain terms that no liberties were to be taken with any guests staying under his roof, though if his own experience was anything to go by he was worrying unnecessarily. Marietta was quite capable of looking after herself, and it was inconceivable that she would encourage Raphael's attentions when she had spurned his.

Jeannette led her guests into the dining-room and the splendidly set table. With relief Marietta saw that Lili had done well.

133

A dazzling white damask cloth set off the silver, and in the centre of the table was a huge roast turkey stuffed with chestnuts and garnished with baked apples. The salads Marietta had taught Lili to make lay appetisingly in their dishes, and on the dresser was a giant bowl of freshly washed fruit.

Jeannette's normally serene face was slightly worried as she turned to her son, saying, 'Henri tells me that the King is already annoyed at the length of your absence.'

'Even Louis cannot expect me to travel south and return in two weeks,' Léon replied, aware that Raphael was whispering in Marietta's ear and that there was a smile lurking at the edge of her lips. He was finding it very hard to keep his attention on his mother's conversation.

'But Jeannette tells me you have no intention of returning at all,' the Duke said, his eyes lingering on the gentle face of the young widow.

'True. My place is here, at Chatonnay, not Versailles. I'm not suited to the life of a courtier.'

'You are not subservient enough for one,' the Duke agreed drily, 'but if Louis wants you back you have no option. I return at the end of the month and he expects you and your wife to accompany me. You will like

Versailles,' he said, speaking to Elise, 'Languedoc is no place for a beautiful woman. At Versailles there are balls and masques and plays...'

'And intrigues and rivalry and adultery,' Léon added.

Raphael took time from flirting with Marietta to raise an eyebrow in his friend's direction. Léon was not known at court for his aversion to rivals and adultery.

'You can't be serious in your decision to remain in Languedoc?' the Duke continued. 'It would be a flagrant disobedience of the King's will.'

At the thought of disobeying the King Elise's hands fluttered so nervously that she spilt her wine. Cécile hurried forward with a napkin and the Duke solicitously poured her a fresh glass. The girl was like a piece of fine china. It was crazy of Léon to keep her in the harsh south when she could be cosseted and pampered at court.

'The King has my absolute loyalty,' Léon replied, wondering what the devil Raphael was saying to Marietta. 'Should he need it, I could summon half the men of Languedoc to fight for him. He has only to ask and I am at his disposal. But my value to the King is as a soldier, not as a fawning courtier. The King is a man like any other. He can command my loyalty, but he cannot rule my life.'

'But that's where you're wrong,' the Duke said heatedly. 'Louis is no ordinary man. Such talk is utter treason, and it's a good thing it is to me you speak such idiocy, and no one else, or you'd end up in the Bastille. The King is the Lord's anointed, an absolute ruler whose word is law. Why, he's semi-divine, and you're treating him as an equal!'

Léon gave a crooked smile. 'Not as an equal, Henri. Simply as a man.'

The Duke groaned and turned to Elise for support. 'Wouldn't you prefer life at Versailles, madame?'

Elise licked her lips nervously. The conversation was completely beyond her. She had understood that after the wedding they were to return to court and she had been looking forward to it. She enjoyed pretty clothes and jewels and music and dancing. The thought of remaining at Chatonnay appalled her, but how could she say so in front of so many people?

The Duke, reading her mind clearly, said triumphantly, 'There, your future bride is all eager for Versailles! She's been buried down here long enough.'

Léon looked across at Elise. 'Is that true? Have you been looking forward to life at Versailles?'

'I … yes…'

'But Chatonnay needs you.'

Elise looked at him blankly. 'But what would I do here? Of what help would I be?'

The question hung painfully in the air. Beneath Léon's piercing gaze Elise was growing more and more uncomfortable. He was talking in riddles, and she did not understand and when his black brows drew together like that he frightened her. She had no way of knowing what he was thinking. He had ridden roughshod over her request for a decent period of mourning. He had not even told her they were not returning to Versailles, and now he said that Chatonnay needed her, and Elise had not the faintest idea of what he meant by such an extra-ordinary remark. Surely all Chatonnay needed was a *châtelaine?*

'Then it *was* you this afternoon,' Raphael de Malbré was saying, his voice full of laughter, his shoulder touching Marietta's as he leaned towards her in the intimacy of a shared secret. His leg too was brushing her skirt. Damn Raphael, but he could be an insolent young pup! Léon thought bad-temperedly, frustrated at Elise's apparent incomprehension of the life they were to lead together and at the way Marietta was responding to Raphael's inanities. The fool had known damn well that it was Marietta driving the cartload of goats, and now he was pouring her wine and their hands were touching...

'No one but a madman would incur the King's wrath for such a triviality,' the Duke continued, unaware that he didn't have his host's full attention. 'There isn't a nobleman in Versailles who wouldn't regard being in the country as a fate worse than death!'

'But they aren't de Villeneuves,' Léon answered quietly.

The Duke leaned his elbows on the table, cradling his silver goblet in his hands. 'The King will not take your disobedience lightly, Léon. For years he has had trouble with the south, uprisings, disturbances. Half the population of Languedoc scarcely regard themselves as Frenchmen. That's why he called you his lion. You have the heart and mind of the south, and if the men of Languedoc are loyal to you, they are loyal to him. It is you they follow to war, not Louis, and he knows it. If he thought your loyalty was in question…' He shrugged expressively.

Elise gave a frightened cry. 'But Léon *is* loyal to the King. Look how he has fought for him!'

The Duke smiled at her reassuringly. 'And the King knows it, madame, and is appreciative. Nevertheless, he commands Léon to return to Versailles, and that old devil Colbert will fill his mind with all sorts of suspicions if Léon disobeys him.'

'But what suspicions?' Elise asked bewilderedly.

'Perhaps that Léon is considering strengthening the hold he has over the men of the south. After all, he must have over two thousand men at his beck and call, and Languedoc with its pestilential Hugeunots is a thorn in Louis' flesh. The only Catholic cities are Toulouse, Carcassonne and Beaucaire. A dangerous situation for any King.'

'But Léon is a good Catholic,' Elise protested. 'He would never take advantage of the Huguenots' loyalty to him.'

'I am well aware of that, madame, but they have followed Léon to war, and such loyalty to a man of different faith is enough to make even a king lose a night's sleep.'

'If you had lived in Paris I would surely have seen you,' Raphael was saying softly at the other end of the table as he leaned towards Marietta, his blue eyes caressing hers.

'Perhaps, monsieur, we lived in different parts of Paris,' Marietta responded, the mischief in her voice belying the ache in her heart. If only it were Léon gazing at her with such adoration! Whose eyes were gleaming with desire, who was so carelessly yet purposefully brushing hands with her as he refilled her glass. But Léon was deep in conversation with the Duke, his betrothed protectively by his side.

'My own father fought for Louis XIII and was in Montpellier when the city walls were pulled down in an effort to keep the Huguenots in check,' the Duke was saying, thinking he had never seen such an angelic face as that of Elise Sainte-Beuve. She brought out in him feelings he had thought long dead. If it wasn't for the fact that she was to be Léon's bride, he was damned if he wouldn't have paid court to her himself.

There was a ripple of laughter from Marietta as Raphael insisted that the only possible reason she hadn't been seen in Paris was because the King had been keeping her to himself. Léon's dark eyes smouldered. Raphael's blatant flirtation with Marietta was bad manners enough, but that she should respond to it...

Jeannette, seeing that Elise was growing more and more unhappy with talk of the King's displeasure, gently suggested that they leave the men to continue the discussion alone while they sought the comfort of the drawing-room. Raphael rose to escort Marietta, but a piercing glance from Léon restrained him and he sat down again, repressing a smile. The girl *was* Léon's mistress. There would be no other reason for his friend's obvious jealousy. To seduce her would not only be the greatest pleasure imaginable, but would also settle a few old scores. He had not forgotten a particularly enchanting Marquis who had forsaken him after only one delicious

140

interlude as soon as Léon had shown an interest in her.

Jeannette sat by the fire with her tapestry, her mind full of Henri's grim warnings as to the King's wrath if Léon stayed away from court. She had no desire to see him leave for the north again, but perhaps it would be for the best. She felt that her son was not seeing his future at Chatonnay clearly. He was envisaging a life with Elise that could never be; Versailles and Paris would suit Elise better than Chatonnay. Perhaps it was better that Léon should recognise that now, even if it did mean saying goodbye to him, perhaps for the last time.

The two young ladies sat together on the settle. Elise only too happy to have Marietta's company, while Céleste sat on the window-seat, fuming at Raphael de Malbré's disinterest in her.

'Oh, what will happen if the King is displeased with Léon?' Elise asked Marietta pathetically, 'and how will we live here? Without the King's favour Léon will have no money, and the land brings in nothing. And I don't *want* to live here. I have no friends, Marietta, no one at all, since my husband died. I was so looking forward to court, and seeing La Valliére and the King!'

'But Versailles is no place to bring up children,' Marietta said gently. 'I know, for I have lived in Paris.'

'Children!' Elise stared at her horrified. 'I can't have children, Marietta. My husband, the Mayor, absolutely forbade it. He said it would kill me!'

Marietta stared at her incredulously. How could she marry Léon and not intend to bear his children? To have Léon's child... The mere thought made Marietta feel faint with longing. To rear his sons at Chatonnay, to hunt and hawk with them. To teach their daughters lace-making. What would she not give to have the chance that Elise was rejecting with such horror?

'And *why* Léon should want to stay here, I can't imagine,' Elise continued, near to tears. 'I thought everything was going to be such fun, with balls and parties.'

Marietta curbed the impatience she felt, remembering that Elise had spent the last six years married to a man old enough to be her grandfather.

'But you will have Léon,' she said, wondering how much more in life any woman could possibly want.

Elise bit her lip. Not even to her new-found friend could she confess that her future husband intimidated her. When he had left Chatonnay he had been a boy, gauche and adoring, now he was supremely self-assured and confident. His zest for life exhausted her, and the traces of the warrior he had become frightened her. As for his love-making... She had protested weakly after his first passionate kiss that it was wrong for her to behave thus with her husband barely cold in his grave, and Léon had reluctantly respected her wishes. But when they were married he would be able to kiss her whenever he pleased and more. Much more.

Elise trembled. How was she to tell him that even after six years of marriage she was still a virgin? That though she craved protection and affection she was unable to respond with any sort of pleasure to more physical advances? And Elise, sheltered though she had been, had wit enough to know that Léon's demands would be very physical indeed.

Tears sprang to the back of her eyes and she twisted her fingers nervously in her lap. It had been so much easier when her husband had been alive. He had only wanted to show her off, to be proud of her, to treat her as a father treats a child. Yet she must marry, for she knew better than anyone else that she was totally unsuited to living life alone – and the instant he had heard of her husband's death hadn't Léon come hot-foot from Versailles to be at her side? He loved her and she would have to strive harder to feel at ease with him. At least this evening they were not alone together. There was Marietta, and the Duke and his son.

When the gentlemen rejoined them, the Duke sat near her and Elise felt herself relax. It was almost like being with her husband again. He made no demands on her and his eyes were kind as well as admiring.

Raphael ignored the warning look Léon gave him, and continued his conversation with Marietta. The more he was with her the more aware he became of something stronger and more elusive than the desire he usually felt when with a beautiful woman. She had an allure that he had never encountered before. No wonder Léon had had the audacity to bring her to Chatonnay with him, to enjoy her company for as long as possible.

With every passing moment Raphael de Malbré's desire for Marietta Riccardi increased and Léon, his friend since childhood, knew it and felt an irrational desire to thrash him. If Raphael de Malbré seduced Marietta it was no concern of his. She could sleep with the stable boy for all he cared. He wasn't in love with her. He was in love with Elise and with difficulty he turned his eyes away from the sight of the fiery red hair and powdered wig indecently close together, and towards her. She was listening entranced to an anecdote of Henri's, and Léon tried to give them his attention. Ever since he had returned he had been cooped up at either Chatonnay or Lancerre. Tomorrow, after visiting Elise, he would go hawking, and if Raphael preferred to play the lovesick fool rather than accompany him he would go alone.

No one noticed Céleste sitting in the window, ignored by Raphael whom she had hoped to charm; ignored even by the Duke. Her mouth was set in a sulky line and she clenched her fists in her lap, determined not to let her disappointment show.

Chapter Six

The next morning Marietta was up at dawn, picking coltsfoot and angelica to make into medicine to take to Ninette Brissac. These few hours every morning, before the rest of the household was awake, were the happiest of Marietta's day. For a short while it was possible to forget Elise and Léon's forthcoming marriage. To forget that soon she would have to leave. Her southern blood loved the rolling sun-baked plains and shrub- and stone-covered hills that surrounded Chatonnay. The orange and terracotta earth, the deep green of the cypress trees as they languished beneath the blazing sun, pleased her far more than the cool greenness of Northern France. Here she felt at home. Here – given a chance – she could have been happy.

'Where are you going to, *ma chérie?*' Raphael de Malbré asked, leaning elegantly against the stable door, barring her way as she went for her horse to make the journey to the Brissacs' cottage.

'To Ninette, with medicine.' Marietta kept her voice cool. She knew very well that Raphael de Malbré was determined to seduce her, and for her pride's sake, when Léon was present, she was glad of his attentions. But on all other occasions she treated him with a coolness that instead of dampening his ardour only succeeded in increasing it.

In Raphael's eyes she was an experienced little minx, blowing hot one minute, cold the next, in order to inflame a man to the point of insanity and so receive for herself far more precious jewels and reimbursements than might normally come her way, though from the way she dressed she paid very little attention to lavish fripperies. Perhaps the little Riccardi was shrewd enough to put the gifts bestowed on her into more tangible assets like land and property. Whatever it was, he was prepared to pay the price. The emerald ring he had offered her the previous evening had been returned with a flush of indignation that indicated that she was used to far more expensive gestures before surrendering her charms. He wondered what price Léon had paid for the favours of a body whose every movement betrayed a sensuality that made his blood race.

That she played the peasant on purpose Raphael had no doubt. It gave her the excuse of showing off her long slender legs when she picked up her skirts to make her way across the kitchen garden, and the sight of her slim feet, almost perpetually bare, was erotic in the extreme. Dressing simply also gave her the excuse to wear her magnificent hair loose and waist-length.

Raphael de Malbré smiled to himself. He wasn't taken in for a moment by Marietta's apparent simplicity. It was as calculated to inflame the senses as the bejewelled and heavy brocades of a courtesan. And far more intriguing and successful.

'A most worthy occupation,' Raphael de Malbré said with amusement. So that was where Léon met his *amoureuse*. 'Perhaps I may accompany you?'

'I think not.' Marietta could not resist a smile as she eyed the pale grey silk of Raphael's tunic and perfection of his garter hose held by a profusion of pink ribbons. 'Saracen is not a horse to ride in such finery, monsieur.'

'I doubt if Saracen is stabled,' Raphael said negligently, eyeing the depths of the stable beyond Marietta's shoulder. Léon's distinctive black stallion was missing, as he knew it would be. He and his rider were already waiting impatiently for the vibrant beauty before him.

Marietta shrugged. 'It makes no difference, monsieur. The roads of Chatonnay are mere tracks and thick with dust. A man needs breeches to ride in Languedoc, not silks and satins.'

'A man needs neither to make love,' Raphael de Malbré said, his voice thickening as he caught her against him, pressing his mouth down hard on hers.

Marietta struggled fiercely. Despite Raphael's dandyism he was young and strong, and there was no escape from his hold as his tongue forced her lips apart, seeking hers avidly.

Saracen was saddled and waiting at the drawbridge for Léon to make an early morning visit to Lancerre. He had returned to the stables only for his riding crop, which he had thrown down in temper after returning from Montpellier with the Duke and Raphael, and struggling in the dirt with Marietta and that damnable goat.

He halted abruptly in the courtyard, his face hardening, a muscle twitching convulsively at his jawline, his hands clenched till the knuckles showed white.

Raphael, Marietta's body at last close against his, his mouth devouring hers, was oblivious of him. Marietta, pushing her hands with all her might against the chest that crushed her, struggling to free her mouth; neither saw nor heard him.

Léon swung on his heel, striding through the château with a look on his face that stopped even his mother in her tracks. He leapt on to Saracen's back, digging his spurs in unnecessarily deep, his mouth set in the harsh, hard line seen only by his adversaries in battle.

'Little whore,' he said beneath his breath as he whipped Saracen the harder. If she had refused his advances in the barn it had only been to heighten his desire. And hadn't she succeeded? After all, there she was, installed at Chatonnay; friend of his mother and virtual mistress of his house. And without him she would be walking the streets of Toulouse, penniless and destitute.

'The Devil take her!' he said angrily to himself as he stormed into the home of the deceased Mayor of Lancerre. What he needed was a day in the saddle, a day hawking and hunting. What did it matter to him if a slut he had known only days should give herself shamelessly to de Malbré? *His* affections were elsewhere. She could go to damnation for all he cared.

Elise trembled visibly as Léon strode into her drawing-room, black brows drawn close together, looking more like a demon from hell than a tender lover. What had happened to put him in such a bad temper? Was it something of her doing? Or something she had not done? Her hands fluttered helplessly. If only the Duke were here to comfort and reassure her; but the Duke was leaving for Versailles after her marriage and then who would she turn to? She felt sick and wondered if she was going to faint but remembered that Léon had little patience for ladies who suffered unnecessarily from the vapours.

She smiled tremulously, hoping to please him; anything if only he wouldn't look so angry, so warlike. She remembered tales of her future husband's prowess on the battlefield and of how he had once killed a man in a duel. He looked very much as if he would like to kill someone now.

Léon paced the feminine drawing-room fretfully. Ever since he had returned home his courtship of Elise had taken place within the confines of this ornately filled room or walking on the terrace outside. He needed exercise. Fresh air.

'Let's hawk,' he said. 'I bought a merlin especially for you.'

Elise blanched. 'I fear I would be poor company...'

'Nonsense!' Léon suppressed his irritation and gave her the benefit of a dazzling smile. 'That's what I came home to Chatonnay for, to hunt and to hawk with my lady love.'

'But I...'

'Come,' Léon drew her to her feet. 'I have a horse that is gentle and quiet and obedient to the lightest touch of the reins. Let's ride into the country and away from watching eyes.' He drew her into his arms and kissed her.

'I could not,' she said, her voice scarcely

audible as she disentangled herself from his embrace. 'I cannot ride, and as for hunting!' She paled. 'A little ride in the carriage, perhaps.'

Léon breathed deeply, hanging on to his self-control with every ounce of his strength. A ride in a carriage! He, the Lion of Languedoc! The most fearless rider and hunter in France! With an enormous effort he smiled, took her hand and kissed it.

'Forgive me, Elise, but I'm in a bad temper and should not have inflicted it upon you. It would be best if I rode by myself today.'

'Oh, yes!' Elise said eagerly and then faltered, hoping she had not sounded too pleased that she was to be robbed of his company.

'Till tomorrow,' he said, wondering whether to take her in his arms and kiss her goodbye. He decided it was not worth it. A kiss as gentle as Elise's left him completely unmoved. The restraints she had imposed on him when he had returned, and which he had thought would be so hard to keep, had been surprisingly easy. He only hoped that once in their marriage bed his expertise in love would be enough to overcome her passivity.

Raphael de Malbré, he thought viciously as he headed Saracen out into the hills, would have had no passivity to overcome in

Marietta; he knew well enough what effect Marietta's kiss had on a man. What effect those kisses had when given freely and passionately was beyond his imagination and he cursed again, trying to console himself with the thought that at least his bride-to-be was chaste and pure, and failing miserably.

At last Marietta managed to free herself from Raphael's mouth and kick him hard enough in the leg to make him gasp with pain and release her.

'How dare you! You *popinjay!*' Marietta spat at him, vaulting on to her mare's back and nearly riding him down in her fury. 'Do you think jewels will buy a Riccardi?'

Raphael leapt hastily to one side as the horse charged past, knocking him on to a bale of straw. He sat there, dazed, removing a scattering of oats from his exquisite apparel. For the first time in his life he had misjudged a woman. Her indignation had been no act. Money and jewels would not buy Marietta's favours so what would? Raphael de Malbré was left with only one answer as he brushed himself down and walked thoughtfully back into the château. Marriage was what the tempestuous little Riccardi was holding out for. Well, she'd lost Léon and had little chance elsewhere with no family and no background to speak of. A pity she wasn't from a family equal in rank to that of the great de Malbrés. The prospect of a lifetime in the bed of that hot-blooded baggage was enough to tempt any man into matrimony.

He rang for his valet to dress the wig that had suffered badly in his escape from the mare's hooves, and then descended the stairs to the more appreciative audience of Céleste. His mind, however, was not on her artless chatter, but on a more serious subject. One that surprised even him.

Marietta rode to the Brissacs' oblivious of the countryside around her. She had been a fool to flirt with Raphael de Malbré and lead him on. At least now he would trouble her no more, or engage her in conversation when Léon's attention was taken up by Elise. For a little while at least, he had saved her pride. Now even that comfort would have to be denied her. But not for long. The wedding was drawing closer with every passing day, and Marietta felt her heart tighten within her as if it would die from lack of air, from lack of love.

Armand ran out to meet her and with difficulty she turned her attention to the sick Ninette, relieved by Armand's assurances that she was responding to the medicine she had given her and that the fever was breaking. Marietta sponged the girl's forehead down with cool water, fed her

155

with the fresh goats' milk she had brought with her and saw that Armand was right. Ninette Brissac was weak and would need several days' more care but she would live. Armand was profuse in his thanks but Marietta merely shrugged. 'Healing is a gift,' she said with a slight smile.

'But you could have died coming to her if it had been smallpox,' Armand protested.

Marietta wondered if Léon would have cared and doubted it. He seemed scarcely aware of her existence.

She had been wrong in thinking that Raphael de Malbré would no longer pay her any attention; instead, his attentions increased. He took no more liberties with her but treated her as a woman of quality and, it seemed to both Jeannette and his father, one whom he was assiduously courting. If Léon had noticed he showed no sign of it and his manner grew terser and curter day by day. He ignored Marietta totally, and when his mother broached the subject, wanting to know the reason why he treated her so unkindly, he was brusque to the point of rudeness. Jeannette could do nothing but watch, worry and wonder.

As Ninette Brissac regained her health Marietta spent more and more time teaching Cécile to make *point de Venise*. Within days her class of one swelled to twenty as the women of Chatonnay came from miles around to sit in the orchard of their *seigneur* and be instructed in the secret art, ages old.

'What the Devil's going on?' Léon asked incredulously as he finished his breakfast and heard the giggles and laughter of a score of women.

'Marietta's lace school,' Jeannette replied equably. She had seen no reason to discuss Marietta's new project with him. He was scarce fit to talk to these days.

'Her *what?*' He threw his napkin to the table and marched to the window. Under the gnarled branches of the apple trees, dark, blonde and grey-haired heads sat over the work in their hands. He recognised young Jacinthe Daudet, the baker's daughter; and Babette, whose mother had died only a year ago; and old Widow Gautier. In the centre was the familiar head of flaming red gold hair.

'Lace school,' Jeannette repeated. 'Marietta is teaching them the art of making *point de Venise*. If she stays long enough and if the women are apt pupils, Marietta will have transformed Chatonnay by bringing prosperity to it at last.'

Léon swallowed. He wanted to be angry with Marietta; anger seemed to be the only safety valve for his feelings. But how could he be angry with a girl who was sharing her most precious skill: a skill held secret, the most valuable thing she possessed, with the women of his village? She had transformed the château. Now she was transforming Chatonnay.

His mother watched him closely as he turned from the window but his eyes were masked of feeling, his face impassive as he picked up his gauntlets and plumed hat, ready for his daily ride to Lancerre.

'This is called a Reprise Bar,' Marietta said to little Jacqueline Pichant, who was only nine and had her tongue stuck determinedly between her teeth. Marietta stretched two threads across a space, passing her needle over and under so the bar was covered in even stitches. 'And this is a Venetian Loop Picot. A Rose Point loop is made by taking a stitch back a little way up the part of the bar you have just made and filling it with buttonhole stitches.'

Jacqueline laboured perseveringly. Marietta turned her attention to Cécile, who was enjoying the warmth of the sun and a respite from Mathilde's scolding.

'This is how we make the pattern,' she said. At that moment there came the sound of hoofbeats over the wooden drawbridge and Marietta felt her heart contract. He was going to Elise again. With difficulty she continued.

'It makes me dizzy when you talk like

that,' Cécile complained after a while.

From the orchard the Lancerre road could be seen clearly, the black stallion with its handsome rider unmistakable.

'Then just watch,' Marietta said, forcing herself to speak. 'See? By varying the number of stitches set close together and the length of spaces, you can make different patterns.' She had lost the girls' attention. Even old Widow Gautier was gazing after the rapidly vanishing figure of Léon de Villeneuve with a dreamy look in her eyes.

'How I wish *I* were the Widow Sainte-Beuve,' Jacinthe said, and the others laughed.

'He'll make a welcome change from the old Mayor of Lancerre, that's for sure,' Thérèse Colet said. 'I doubt if he even managed more than a goodnight kiss!'

'She'll get more than that from the *Comte*,' Jacinthe said, and there was another burst of ribald laughter. Marietta kept her head firmly lowered over her work, her cheeks flushed, her eyes agonised.

'Do you remember how he threatened to kill the Mayor when he first heard about the marriage?' Babette said reminiscently. 'And how it took his father and over a dozen men to stop him?'

'And how he said he would return for her, even if it meant waiting years and years and years?'

They sighed rapturously. Cécile giggled. 'Armand told me that all the ladies at Versailles were in love with him.'

'Not the Queen as well?' they chorused incredulously.

'Why not the Queen?' Jacinthe asked. 'She's a woman, isn't she? *I'm* in love with him, and I would be even if I were Queen.'

'And a fat lot of good it would do you,' her sister said as she finished marking out her pattern. 'You can't even get the swineherd to fall in love with you!'

The other girls tittered, knowing full well how infatuated Jacinthe was with Nicholas Sandeau, and how he ignored her.

'I overheard the Duke telling Madame that Madame Francine Beauvoir was the *Comte*'s mistress when he was at court,' Cécile ventured. 'I bet that's why he does not want to return there with his new bride. And he doesn't, Armand told me so.'

'I heard that he fought a duel over her,' Jacinthe added. 'I wonder what it would be like to be fought over? She must be very beautiful.'

'So is Madame Sainte-Beuve,' said Babette loyally. '*She*'s the love of his life. He must love her very much to have returned for her after so many years.'

The rest of them agreed that he must.

With immense effort Marietta continued as if they had never been interrupted. 'Now,

Jacqueline, trace a single thread over your finished outline, fixing it in place by passing frequent stitches over it.'

The girls returned their attention to their work and Cécile and Lili had the grace to blush at the way they had spoken of the Comte in front of a girl who, after all, was no servant but a guest. And, if rumours were to be believed, perhaps something more.

Léon spent an unsatisfactory day making small talk with Elise in the claustrophobic atmosphere of her garden. He felt relieved when she made no objection that he spent the next day hunting again. On returning to Chatonnay and finding Marietta and Raphael deep in a game of chess, he had even had the grace to thank her for the instruction she was giving to his peasants.

Marietta had struggled to regain her composure and barely looked up from the game, knowing she could not meet those dark eyes without the emotion in her own showing clearly.

Léon poured himself a glass of wine and spent the evening in conversation with the Duke and Jeannette, glancing with ever-increasing intervals across the room to where Raphael and Marietta continued to play. He noticed that Raphael was having to concentrate hard and he frowned. Where the devil had she learned to play a game of chess that challenged a de Malbré? And why was it Raphael who was enjoying such a diversion? He himself loved the game, but when he had suggested teaching Elise she had paled with horror, protesting that she would never understand such a complicated pastime and that all but the simplest game of cards was beyond her.

Marietta, becoming more and more aware of Léon's gaze, allowed Raphael to win and excused herself. To be in the same room and not to be able to talk and laugh or have the empathy with him that she had felt in those first heady hours after he had rescued her, was becoming more and more of a physical impossibility. That he would never love her she knew, but she longed for him to like her a little. To smile at her. Talk to her. She leaned her aching head against the coolness of the window, gazing sightlessly out over the dark trees as they soughed in the night air. Her days seemed composed of manœuvres to avoid him, to save herself some measure of suffering. In the morning she would ride early to see Ninette Brissac. By the time she returned Léon would have ridden to Lancerre, and another meeting would be avoided. She lay down in her bed, but sleep was a long time coming.

Léon awoke with a feeling of unacknowledged relief. Today he could dress for riding and not for courting. It made a pleasant change and it put him in a better mood than he had been in for days. The church bells were ringing the Angelus as he strode across the flags in the courtyard to the stables and Saracen.

Marietta, returning from the Brissacs' cottage, rode full tilt into him. 'God's truth!' he exclaimed, leaping out of the way. 'Are you forced to ride as if you're fleeing a thousand devils?'

'No, but I've work to do.' She hadn't meant to sound rude, but her skirt was covered in dust from the road and the breeze had dishevelled her hair. It seemed that she was always seen at a disadvantage, especially in comparison to the exquisite perfection of Elise.

'Never mind the work,' Léon said impulsively. 'Let's fly the hawks,' and without even waiting for her assent spurred Saracen in the direction of the drawbridge. Marietta's hesitation was fractional. It was the first time since her arrival at the château that he had spoken to her in the old free and easy manner. Digging in her heels she rode after him, the church bells were still ringing as they galloped between the thatched cottages of the village and out into the stone and shrub covered hills surrounding it. Saracen's tail streamed in the wind and the sheer speed of her own horse took Marietta's breath away as she strove to narrow the gap between them.

Léon rode fiercely, giving Saracen full rein, feeling a sense of heady breathlessness as the stifling boredom of the last few days was forgotten. Once again he enjoyed the feel of a galloping horse beneath him, the sight of a limitless horizon, and ahead of him his stable boy waiting obediently with the dogs and hawks. The dogs strained at their leashes as he wheeled Saracen round, his eyes alight as Marietta spurred her mare the last few yards.

'You ride like a man!'

White teeth flashed in a smile Marietta had begun to think she had only dreamed about. It was the highest compliment Léon could give a woman, and knowing it Marietta laughed, feeling a sense of elation. Just when she had given up hope the old empathy had sprung up between them once more. But only for a short time. Tomorrow he would be with Elise. In a week she herself would be in Montpellier or Narbonne, but for the moment they were together and it was enough.

Her face was radiant and the stable boy gazed at her with such adoration that Léon drew his brows quickly together and ordered him to unhood the birds. 'Have you hawked before?' he asked Marietta, already knowing the answer. There were times when he wondered if there was anything she had not done or could not do.

'Not since my father died.' Her flamboyant red-gold hair fell loosely over her shoulders, her breasts heaving with the exertion of the ride.

Léon's breath caught in the back of his throat. By the Mass, but she was a beauty. No trinkets, no powder, no paint – just satin-smooth skin, sparkling eyes that made a man feel good to be alive and a vibrant vitality that paled every other woman into insignificance.

'Then take the merlin.'

The bird had been bought especially for Elise, but Léon knew that his future wife would never ride with it on her wrist. There was a tinkle of bells as the birds moved their legs in the jesses and then the boy had slipped the merlin, the plumes on its feet fluttering lightly in the faint breeze. They reminded Marietta of the way Léon's exotic hat of ostrich plumes swayed elegantly when he rode off to Lancerre. She liked him better without his finery, his body strong and forceful, dressed for riding and for action, the powerful muscles of his arms and chest showing beneath his linen shirt as he slipped his falcon.

The bird flew at once, so high that Marietta had to shield her eyes against the glare of the sun. Then, so suddenly that

Marietta gasped, it plummeted seizing its prey. The stable boy unleashed the eager dogs and they ran, noses to the wind, to retrieve the hare that would eventually grace their master's table.

The merlin brought down a lark and a pigeon, and the dogs yapped merrily at their heels as they rode higher and higher into the hills, leaving the stable boy far behind them. This was better than the lush woods surrounding Versailles, thronged with lords and ladies of the court, more anxious to be seen in the King's presence than in enjoying their sport.

At last Léon hooded his hawk and rested his hands on the pommel of his saddle, feasting his eyes on the land around him.

'Who would prefer Paris or Versailles to this?' he asked Marietta, his dark eyes gleaming with an expression she had never seen before.

The love he felt for the sun-parched land was tangible and Marietta responded to it fully. 'Not me,' she answered.

He looked across at her, at the flush that heightened the honey-gold of her cheeks, at the rapturous expression on her face as she viewed the rolling land of vines and figs that was his. She was a southerner by blood and by nature. It was little wonder that she had never fitted into life at Evray: never been happy there. Sensing his gaze upon her she turned, this time no longer afraid to meet his gaze.

The green eyes burned so fiercely that it seemed to Léon no man could look into their depths without feeling the heat. The desires and emotions he had been fighting ever since he returned with her to Chatonnay could be fought no longer. His heart began to beat in slow thick strokes as he slid from his saddle. He must have her. If he did not she would for ever be a fever in his blood, inflaming and tormenting him. Once possessed, surely he could forget her as he had so many others? Slowly, without taking his gaze from hers, he crossed to her mare and circled her waist with his hands.

Her heart racing, Marietta allowed his hands to close around her, their heat searing through the thin cambric of her bodice as if she were naked. He lifted her down to her feet, holding her so close against him that Marietta could feel his heart beating against hers.

'Marietta ... Marietta...' His voice was thick against her hair and then his mouth sought hers with increasing urgency. Every nerve in her body responded to the touch of his hands, the pleasure of his lips on hers and then, as he cupped her breasts and as she felt the hardness of his body against hers and her own shameless desire, she uttered a helpless cry, twisting her head away from his.

'Elise! What of Elise!' she demanded, and at the fleeting incomprehension in his eyes she knew the truth. He was still going to marry Elise. He was not making love to her. He was taking her as any man would a willing servant girl. And she, Marietta Riccardi, had been on the verge of submitting. Hot tears scalded her eyes as she drew back her palm and slapped Léon de Villeneuve with all the force she could muster, across the cheek.

His desire changed to incredulity and then to anger.

'What the devil...?'

With a cruelty he had not known he was capable of, he crushed her to him, bringing his mouth down so hard on hers that he tasted blood. Vainly she struggled as he forced her down on the ground, the weight of his body pinioning hers.

'No,' she gasped, as his mouth sought her throat, her breasts. 'Not like this, Léon! For the love of God! Not like this!'

With one hand he secured her flailing wrists while with the other he tore open the bodice of her gown. Marietta moaned and Léon halted, panting fiercely.

'Don't play the virgin with me, Marietta. You were not quite so reluctant for Raphael's attentions!'

'No,' she shook her head vainly, hardly able to breathe. 'He tried to kiss me once but nothing more.'

'And so to spurn him you laugh and flirt and play chess?' Léon said savagely.

'And if I do?' Marietta's eyes flashed fire. 'And if I had accepted his kiss, what of it? Raphael de Malbré is not a man about to be married!'

Her words were more effective than any show of violence could have been. He hurled her away from him so savagely that she rolled for yards in the dust and dirt. Then, with an oath, he sprang to his feet and strode towards Saracen without even bothering to give her a backward glance or brush the earth from his breeches.

'Léon!' she called after him, her voice anguished. 'Léon!'

But the black stallion was already disappearing down the hillside in a flurry of scattered pebbles.

Chapter Seven

The sun was beginning to set when Marietta returned at last to the château, the white stone walls golden in the last light of day. Her heart contracted when she saw the team of ebony-black horses and the elegant carriage that announced the presence of Elise. She entered by the kitchen door, hurrying discreetly to her bed-chamber to bathe and change. Cécile eyed her curiously, noting the torn bodice of her gown. The Comte, too, had arrived back at Chatonnay like a man who had spent the day wrestling in the dirt. It was all very intriguing.

She provided Marietta with a bowl of rose-scented water, noting with interest the bruises on Marietta's wrists. Hurriedly she excused herself and ran to find Lili. They had been together, the Comte and Mariette. Armand himself had seen them ride off into the hills and from the way she had returned … Cécile's plump cheeks were pink with excitement. That her betters should behave as she did was a constant source of wonder to her. Especially when she thought of the Comte, now elegant in black velvet, his buttonholes heavily embroidered with gold thread, paying court to the Widow Sainte-Beuve. Cécile was sure *that* lady had never known the pleasure of having her bodice ripped open or her wrists bruised by an over-eager lover.

Elise was happier than she had been for a long time. At last she had persuaded Léon to wait a little while longer before marrying her. The *Abbé* had been as shocked as she herself had been at the thought of her remarrying within weeks of her husband's death.

To her surprise and relief Léon had not argued. Another few weeks would make no difference. The urgency he had felt on first returning was now lost in a welter of emotions that he was powerless to understand. When Marietta, unable to stay away any longer from the drawing-room without seeming to display bad manners, had finally descended the stairs and joined them, he had turned his back on her pointedly, engaging the Duke in deep discussion.

Marietta licked dry lips and forced a smile in Jeannette's direction. Jeannette, even more curious about her son's and her guest's activities than Lili or Cécile, smiled back, patting the seat beside her. Raphael, ensconced with Céleste in the window, was unable to join her as he wished. Another few minutes and then he would have done his duty by Léon's cousin and be free to drink in the sight of Marietta, her red-gold hair brushed into a semblance of order, her simple gown transformed by her natural grace. Her feet, as always when they dined, were slippered in velvet as Céleste's and Madame Sainte-Beuve's. He preferred them bare, and felt a rush of heat to his groin as the vision of a completely naked Marietta arose before him.

'*Please* say you'll do it for me,' Elise was saying, her small hand reaching out for Marietta's. 'It would mean such a lot to me. I shall never have the chance of such a gown again, not even if we go to court, for the Duke tells me that a gown of *point de Venise* would cost thousands of livres.'

'But I couldn't, Elise. There isn't time.'

'Then only the bodice. Oh, *please*, Marietta! Please say you will.'

Marietta looked into the pleading blue eyes helplessly. How could she possibly make Elise's wedding gown after the scene that had just taken place between herself and Léon? Yet how could she refuse? To do so would seem churlish in the extreme.

'I've seen the collar you made for Jeannette and it's exquisite. *Please*, Marietta. It would make me so happy.'

Marietta sought for an excuse that would be acceptable and failed to find one. 'All

173

right,' she said at last, 'but I doubt I'll be able to finish a whole gown, Elise.'

'Oh, the bodice alone would be enough. I could fit it on to a skirt of heavy satin.' She clapped her hands with joy. 'Oh, Léon! Marietta has promised to make me my wedding gown!'

Léon turned to his future bride, a tiny nerve throbbing at his temple. 'If it pleases you, my love.'

'Of course it pleases me! It will be the finest gown in the whole of Languedoc. Oh you are kind, Marietta. I do wish you would promise to stay in Chatonnay instead of returning to Venice.'

Léon kept his eyes determinedly averted from Marietta and the Duke, like so many others, began to wonder. Léon's reputation with women was notorious, yet the Duke, who had known him since he was a child, would have sworn that when it came to marriage Léon would have entered into that contract with loyalty. He had been right when he had said he was no courtier. The morals of the court might have suited Léon in his single state, but where his marriage was concerned he would be as old-fashioned as his father had been, loving one woman and one woman only. Yet he was sure he saw an agony of longing in Léon's dark eyes whenever they rested on the Riccardi girl.

Puzzled, he turned his attention to the fair-headed vision in ice-blue silk, receiving a smile that would melt the hardest heart.

'What about some music?' Raphael asked, finally disentangling himself from Céleste's attentions. 'I've yet to hear that spinet play.'

'It does, I assure you,' Jeannette said with a laugh. 'There's nothing I would like better than to hear it played.'

Céleste longed to suggest that she should play, but she knew that if she did so, instead of shining in Raphael's eyes, she would only show herself to be a provincial. Her playing was not of a high enough standard for a man used to the accomplishments of court women.

Raphael's garter hose fitted indecently tight, bunches of ribbon at his knees and at the shoulders of his silk doublet. In his high-heeled shoes of scarlet leather Céleste thought him even more magnificent than the King himself, but his eyes were no longer on her. They were on Marietta, the question in them clear but unspoken.

Slowly Marietta rose to her feet. Why not? It would do Léon de Villeneuve good to see that the Riccardis were brought up as ladies of accomplishment. That he had made a grave error in treating her as a peasant. She felt a tightening of her stomach muscles as she approached the spinet. It had been ten long years since she had last played, not

175

since her father had been alive and they had lived in comfort. She sat herself at Jeannette's spinet, every eye in the room on her. To all of them she was an enigma. If she could play, then the breeding she displayed in her every action would prove to be no play-acting. The Riccardis must have been as high-born as Marietta claimed.

Jeannette felt a sudden wave of apprehension and knotted her hands in her lap, whispering a silent prayer. Only Céleste and Elise were happily oblivious of the sudden tension. Marietta raised her hands, and the Duke's eyes narrowed speculatively. Raphael's willed her to prove to them all that Marietta Riccardi was fit to marry a de Malbré, while Léon's were unreadable.

The music came pure and sweet, every note perfect, and Marietta allowed herself a small smile of satisfaction as she heard the intake of breath around her: the Duke and Léon surprised, Raphael and Jeannette relieved.

'Can we dance?' Céleste asked eagerly. 'Oh, please let us dance.'

The Duke, nothing loth, rose to his feet and held out his hands to Elise. Elise blushed prettily and accepted. Raphael had no option but to proffer his hand to Céleste.

With hands held high the two couples moved down the length of the vast drawing-room in the stately steps of a minuet. Apart, together, apart. The Duke felt like a man twenty years his junior. Reluctantly as the music ended, he returned Elise to her future husband. Céleste remained firmly on Raphael's arm as Marietta began to play again.

Léon made a move to join his friend and cousin, but Elise protested with a little laugh and a flutter of her fan. 'One dance is enough! I am quite breathless.'

The Duke solicitously poured her a glass of reviving wine and proceeded to tell her she danced like an angel.

Raphael, frustrated at dancing and not being able to hold Marietta's hand in his, asked Céleste if she could sing.

'As sweetly as a nightingale,' Jeannette assured him and so it was that Céleste found herself given the opportunity to show off her own accomplishments, but only so that Raphael could dance with Marietta.

And Marietta did not tire as easily as Elise Sainte-Beuve. Refusing to let Léon see the pain he had caused her, she laughed and danced with Raphael, her velvet-slippered feet as light on the floor of the drawing-room as they were nimble in the kitchen garden. Raphael, eyes alight, laughed down at her. She was a delight; accomplished, graceful, passionate. A constant source of surprise and wonderment. He would marry her, and be damned with the sniggers of the court. They would stop soon enough when she had charmed the King and she would do that as easily as she had charmed him.

All too soon Céleste protested she could sing no longer and Raphael reluctantly parted hands with Marietta. He would propose tonight, he resolved. They could be married before they returned to Paris.

Léon escorted Elise to her carriage, placing a gentle kiss on the forehead of her upturned face. Elise felt reassured. This kind of attention she could submit to. The passionate kisses he had forced upon her earlier, and which had so frightened her, had only been because of the years they had been parted; a last remnant of his roistering days at court. They would not occur again. Elise felt happy at the thought.

'I envy you,' the Duke said sincerely as Léon returned to the drawing-room and Elise's coach and six had thundered away down the drive. 'She's utter perfection. You're a lucky man, Léon.'

A brief smile twisted Léon's mouth as he accepted the Duke's congratulations, his attentions elsewhere. It was on Marietta and Raphael, who were nowhere to be seen. The torches flickered in the iron rungs on the wall, illuminating the passage in a soft light as Raphael de Malbré asked Marietta Riccardi to be his wife. She gazed at him uncomprehendingly, and he laughed softly taking her hand and palm upwards kissing it.

'I've learnt my lesson, *ma chére*. No more trying to tumble you in the hay, only in a marriage bed.'

He drew her confidently into the circle of his arms, kissing her with increasing fervour. For a moment Marietta was so numbed by shock that she was unable to react, and when she did so it was to pull herself determinedly away from his embrace. Undaunted, he tenderly traced the outline of her cheek with his finger.

'What a beauty you are, *ma chére*. What a sensation you will be in dresses of gold and silver at Versailles.'

She shook her head. 'Versailles is not for me, Raphael. And I can never marry you.'

He smiled, his fingers moving to the softness of her lips. 'Because your family is not known? You have said yourself that the Riccardis are noble and they are also beautiful.' His hands slid around her waist pulling her close. 'Breathtakingly beautiful, *ma chére*.'

She said quietly, 'I don't love you, Raphael.'

This time he paused, his eyes searching hers. It had never occurred to him that she would have been anything but delighted at accepting a proposal of marriage from a de Malbré.

'That one of us is marrying for love is miracle enough,' he said at last. 'Let me assure you, *ma petite,* that once married and in my bed you will soon overcome your reluctance.'

She shook her head again but Raphael only smiled.

'Sleep on your doubts. They will vanish like the night.'

Behind them could be heard the sound of approaching footsteps and Raphael, intending to kiss her once more, reluctantly let her go and turned to meet Jeannette's curious gaze. Marietta made her escape and Jeannette said with unaccustomed coolness, 'I hope I was mistaken in what I saw, Raphael.'

'Indeed you were not, madame, but there is no need to distress yourself. My intentions are strictly honourable.'

'They did not look honourable to me,' Jeannette said bluntly. It was bad enough entertaining doubts about Marietta and Léon, without finding her in Raphael's arms as well.

'I have just asked your enchanting guest to be my wife,' Raphael said, enjoying Jeannette's look of complete stupefaction and then delight.

'Oh, Raphael! That's wonderful! I've been so worried about her – where she would go, what she would do.'

'She will go to Versailles, madame. As for what she will do...' Raphael's eyes gleamed suggestively, but Jeannette was too happy at having Marietta's future secured to scold him for his impudence.

'Why such scenes of joy?' Léon asked as he approached them, his tunic jacket slung negligently over his shoulder and hanging by his finger, his shirt already open to the waist as he made his way to his bed.

'Marietta is to marry Raphael!'

Too late Jeannette realised that her son might not share her pleasure in such a fact.

'Is that true?'

Not a muscle of Léon's face moved. He was like a man turned to stone.

'Quite true,' Raphael leaned against the wall, savouring the moment to the full. Léon should never have tried to ride two horses at the same time. Marrying the milk-and-water Widow Sainte-Beuve for respectability and keeping Marietta for enjoyment had been nothing but sheer greed. Raphael felt a sense of supcriority for the first time over his friend. He himself didn't care a fig for respectability. He was going to marry her, and to hell with what the gossips said. For once he had shown himself more fearless than Léon.

'Then I wish you well,' Léon said through clenched teeth, and without more ado nodded a curt goodnight to his mother and strode off down the candlelit passage to his room. Seconds later there came the angry slamming of a door that both Raphael and Jeannette pretended not to hear.

Later, leaving Raphael to explain his decision to his appalled father, Jeannette wrapped a shawl over her nightdress and tiptoed softly towards her son's room. They had to talk. She had to know what his feelings were. What was happening to change him from the laughing, devil-may-care son she had known into the brooding, taciturn figure that sat silently for hours staring into the flames of the fire?

His candles were lit, the light seeping beneath the door. Jeannette raised her hand to knock and paused. There came the distinct sound of a decanter against glass and the pouring of liquid, and then a chair fell as he stumbled across the room. There was no point in talking to Léon. He was too drunk to talk. Too drunk to see anything but the image of Marietta Riccardi – naked and abandoned in Raphael de Malbré's bed.

The next morning Marietta avoided both Léon and Raphael by summoning Lili and Cécile for their lacemaking lesson at an unusually early hour. The sun was already warm, drying the dew on the grass and promising another day of sun and endless blue skies. The village women had not yet appeared, and the orchard was unusually quiet as the girls bent diligently over their work and Marietta began to make the lace that was to become Elise Sainte-Beuve's wedding gown.

Cécile and Lili spoke softly between themselves from time to time, but Marietta became gradually unaware of them. A strange sensation crept over her as she gazed into the distance. She no longer saw the orchard and hills beyond, but the church of Chatonnay and Léon and his bride standing hand in hand, the bride radiant as she wore a gown of *point de Venise* lace, the relief so beautiful that it looked like sculpture. Her face was unseen, hidden by her veil, but she could see Léon clearly. Tall and strong, jet-black curls hanging freely to his shoulder, dressed in a tunic of scarlet velvet edged with gold braid, his knee-high boots gleaming, his sword at his side.

She felt a tightness around her chest so that she thought she was going to faint. It was like being caught up in a tunnel of unbearable light. The seasons changed. The leaves falling; flowers growing. The pews of the church were more lavish, a gilded crucifix that had not been there before now hung above the altar. The bride was young, no more than seventeen. She had Léon's dark eyes and thick lashes and a full, generously curved mouth. Her mother's dress fitted her to perfection as she stood, hand in hand before the priest who was to perform the marriage. Marietta felt a love beyond all bearing for this girl who was Léon's daughter; this girl who was marrying in Chatonnay's church wearing the gown that she, Marietta, was now making.

And then, through the mists of time, another girl stood in her place. Small and with rosy cheeks that dimpled when she laughed. The lace dress looked more delicate now; it had been wrapped for so many years, carefully protected from the light.

She had thought she would leave Chatonnay and that she would never more be part of Léon's life or he of hers. Now she knew that she was wrong. Elise's wedding gown would be a family heirloom. Léon's daughter would wear it when she took her marriage vows, and his granddaughter. As long as Léon de Villeneuve lived he would be reminded of her. When those glossy black curls turned to grey and then to white, he would stand in Chatonnay's church and see his merry-faced granddaughter married to the man she loved, and the dress she wore would be the dress that she, Marietta Riccardi, had made.

The merry face of Léon's granddaughter slowly faded and once more she saw the orchard and the rolling hills beyond, shining in the early morning heat haze. Cécile and Lili were talking together in low voices. Above her head, in the boughs of the apple tree, a linnet sang. Marietta felt an incredible sense of peace and tranquillity. She knew now what the future held. It was a life without Léon, and there would never be another love for her. Yet she would remain a part of him, and it seemed to Marietta that she could ask for nothing more.

Mathilde angrily shooed the dogs away from the kitchen door, vexed at having to bake the bread and make the breakfast herself while Cécile and Lili idled in the orchard.

'You'd best go back to the kitchen until the village women come. Then we will continue,' Marietta said, picking up her needle. The gown she had seen in her vision had been a full-length gown of *point de Venise*, not a lace bodice over a satin skirt. She had no time to lose.

Reluctantly the girls returned to the chores in the kitchen and Marietta continued to work, the only sound being that of an occasional bird and the hum of the bees from the nearby hives. She was disturbed by Céleste picking her way delicately across the grass, her gown raised high to protect its hem, slippered feet tiptoeing so as not to become spoiled or grass-stained.

'What on earth are you doing out so early?

Mathilde tells me you've been up since dawn.'

'I couldn't sleep.'

Marietta was sitting on the grass as Cécile and Lili had been, her legs and feet bare. Céleste found it hard to believe that she was the same person who had played the spinet and danced so entrancingly the night before. So far she was in happy ignorance of Raphael's intention of marrying Marietta but not of his interest in her. Why should he prefer Marietta to herself? *She* never behaved in an unseemly fashion. Yet he had danced far more the previous evening with Marietta than he had danced with her. And it was always to Marietta that his eyes returned.

Life was really very unfair, and much as she liked Marietta, Céleste wished she would pack her bags and continue on her journey to Venice, or Montpellier or Narbonne. Anywhere, just as long as it gave her the opportunity to ensnare Raphael de Malbré without competition.

'Léon is already preparing to leave for Lancerre,' she said, watching Marietta's face curiously. 'It seems he can barely tear himself away from Madame Sainte-Beuve's side.'

'Which is just as it should be, as he is to marry her,' Marietta replied composedly.

Céleste could not detect a flicker of

jealousy on Marietta's heart shaped face yet she was sure there was something between her cousin and the girl he had brought home with him. In public he barely acknowledged her, yet even that was curious, for Léon was a notorious charmer and Céleste had never seen him behave towards any woman with the indifference he displayed towards Marietta, and even Céleste had to grudgingly admit that she was a woman any man would go out of his way to entertain. Raphael de Malbré was smitten by her, and that alone was testimonial enough of her charms.

The Lancerre road ran perilously close to the orchard, and Marietta had no desire to see or be seen by Léon. 'I think it's time I went to visit Ninette,' she said, picking her work up carefully.

'But surely she's cured now? Armand is back at the château and says his daughter is stronger and healthier than ever before.'

'Nevertheless I think I will see her,' Marietta repeated firmly, and then broke off as Céleste screamed, frozen in horror. An adder was weaving with lightning speed towards them through the grass. Marietta moved instinctively backwards, her skirt caught high, but before she could spring to her feet the deadly head rose, the poisonous fangs sinking deep into the flesh above her knee.

Céleste's screams rang on and on, her fists clenched tightly to her chest, too horrified for coherent thought. The snake curled with lightning speed back into the thick grass, leaving Marietta white-faced, her eyes staring terrified at the deadly mark on her thigh.

'Stop it!' she said desperately to Céleste. 'Stop screaming! Suck the poison out. Now! Quickly!'

Céleste's eyes were uncomprehending, her screams rising to mindless hysteria. Helplessly, Marietta knew that she would gain no help from Céleste and there were only minutes in which she could save her life. Vainly she tried to reach the fang marks herself, but it was impossible. She was dying. Dying before she had made the de Villeneuve wedding gown.

'Help! Léon! For the love of God!'

Céleste saw the familiar horse and rider taking to the Lancerre road, and the sight brought her back to her senses. She ran towards him, stumbling in her haste, her cries rending the still morning air.

Léon reined in immediately. He was aware of Céleste racing headlong towards him, her mouth a gaping hole as she screamed again for help and of Marietta lying in the grass behind her. Fear gripped him and he wheeled Saracen round, jumping the wall that separated the lane from the orchard, weaving between the trees, vaulting from the saddle to her side as Céleste gasped, 'She's been bitten by a snake!'

Marietta was barely conscious, her face white. 'I can't reach,' she panted. 'The poison needs sucking out...'

Léon seized her bare leg in his hand, the black curled head bent low as he kneeled beside her, sucking at the fang-marks and spitting viciously into the grass while Céleste grasped the trunk of an apple tree for support.

Céleste's screams had been heard in the château. Mathilde was already breathlessly running towards them, Raphael and the Duke bursting from the doorway. The wound was clean; her leg was still held in his hands and for the first time in his life Léon de Villeneuve was shaking from the aftermath of fear.

'Léon... Léon...' Feebly she reached towards him, trying to sit up.

'What the devil! Marietta! Are you all right? What happened?'

Raphael de Malbré was seizing her shoulders, dragging her away from Léon's hold, lifting her in his arms.

'A snake,' Léon said, still kneeling on the grass, unable to move.

'Sweet Jesus.' Raphael de Malbré turned and began to run towards the château, a semi-conscious Marietta in his arms.

Léon remained where he was, kneeling on the grass, shaken by a terror he had never felt, not even in the heat of battle. At last, ashen-faced, he rose to his feet and made his way slowly to where Saracen pawed the ground. There was no sense in remaining at Chatonnay. There was nothing more he could do for her. Raphael had shown him that all too clearly, in the proprietorial manner he had taken her from his hold and carried her back to the château.

He headed Saracen away from Lancerre and into the hills. There could be no seeing Elise today. He wanted only to be with Marietta and he could not, nor did he have the right. She was to be Raphael de Malbré's wife, and Léon knew that it was he who had driven her into his friend's arms.

Marietta was as distraught at being taken so abruptly from Léon's grasp as she had been at the snake bite. He had saved her life. She had seen the expression of sheer terror on his face as he had raced towards her, terror because she, Marietta, was in danger. If only Raphael had not come and Mathilde, bustling about with good intentions, then maybe … maybe…

Weakly she closed her eyes. Mathilde had tucked her up in bed and closed the heavy curtain. The room was dark and cool. At her side sat Raphael, his face anxious, his hand holding hers. She had not the strength to ask him to leave. She wanted no one but Léon, would never want anyone but Léon.

It was his father, who silently, by the lightest touch on his shoulder, indicated to him that he should leave. Marietta, aware of the closing of the door, opened her eyelids.

'I wanted to talk to you,' the Duke said, leaning on his ebony-topped cane. 'Are you strong enough?'

'Quite strong enough.' She sat up against the pillows. 'It was the shock that made me so weak.' And the sight of Léon's face, terror-stricken, bending over her, his mouth on her flesh, sucking out the venom, heedless of anything but her safety.

'Good. Perhaps we could have a little more light.'

'With pleasure.'

The Duke himself drew back the blinds, bathing the room in sunshine.

'I have a very painful duty to perform, Mademoiselle Riccardi.' Slowly he turned and walked back towards the bed, the sunlight flashing on the diamonds in the heels of his shoes. 'Raphael tells me that he has asked for your hand in marriage. He acted rashly and in haste, and it is my sad obligation to tell you that no such wedding can ever take place.'

'I know.' The colour had returned to Marietta's cheeks and there was the hint of a smile about her mouth.

191

The Duke paused, wondering if he had heard right. 'The difficulty is in the stations of our families,' he continued.

'That is of no account,' Marietta interrupted spiritedly. 'The Riccardis are fit enough to marry where they please.'

'Not in this case,' the Duke answered gravely.

'In this case,' Marietta said, something of the old mischief back in her eyes, 'they do not desire to.'

The Duke frowned, slightly, staring down at her. The de Malbrés were one of the noblest families in France, and this little baggage had managed to inflame his experienced and sophisticated son to the point of proposing marriage – and now, when he came to deliver the dreadful blow that she, a Riccardi, would never become the Duchesse de Malbré, she simply shrugged and smiled and said she had no such desire in the first place. He had expected hysteria, threats, protests. Anything but this careless indifference.

'Are you quite sure that you have understood what I have been saying to you, mademoiselle?'

'You have been saying that I cannot marry Raphael. It is *you,* Monsieur le Duc, who seems not to understand our conversation. I told your son when he asked me that I would not marry him. He, like you, seems to put very little belief in my words.'

'But, my dear child, why?' Henri mopped his forehead with a cologne-soaked kerchief. Really, this conversation was taking a most unexpected turn.

'Because I do not love him,' Marietta said simply.

Henri clutched tightly at his cane for support. Mother of God, the little chit was turning down marriage with the great de Malbrés because she did not love! It was unbelievable!

'And so you see, Monsieur le Duc, you had no reason to put yourself to such distress.'

'No. Quite.' Henri felt immensely relieved and vaguely disconcerted. That a young lady of dubious background should *refuse* marriage with a de Malbré! Surely his family had been insulted?

'Perhaps you would tell Jeannette I will be down for dinner,' Marietta said, a smile playing at the corner of her mouth as she sensed the thoughts chasing through her distinguished visitor's head. 'I feel quite myself again.'

The Duke said that he would, reflecting as he descended the broad sweep of the stairs that he had, in effect, been summarily dismissed and felt a glass of brandy was called for.

By the time Marietta came down for dinner – dressed in the amber velvet gown that so accentuated her beauty – the rest of the household was already seated. Léon kept his gaze firmly averted from hers. Raphael revelled in the sight of her, still confident that despite his father's displeasure he would have Marietta for his wife.

'I must say I'm quite enjoying this retreat from the clamour of the court,' the Duke said, relishing the rare delicacy of fresh oysters. 'It's enough to turn a man into a recluse.'

Jeannette eyed her old friend's lavishly embellished doublet and laughed. 'Another month of it and you would die of boredom, Henri.'

'I assure you I would not. I have never known the days pass so quickly.'

Jeannette paused and then said lightly, watching her son's face, 'It's Elise who has done that for you. You spend more time with her even than Léon.'

There was the merest touch of heightened colour in the Duke's face. Léon continued to stare moodily into his wine-glass. 'Madame Sainte-Beuve likes to hear of Versailles and I like to talk to her about it. The new fashions interest her greatly.'

'And me,' Céleste interrupted as they moved from the dining table to the main drawing-room. 'I've heard that even La

194

Valliére wears a patch on her face. Is that true? And does she wear it *passionée* or *gallante?*'

'La Valliére does not wear a patch at all,' the Duke said, smiling across the candlelit room to where Céleste literally hung on the edge of her chair waiting for gossip of Versailles. 'She is beautiful enough without.'

'Is that true?' Céleste turned to where Marietta sat a little apart from them, busy with her lace.

'Quite true. She leaves such fashions to the likes of Madame de Montespan.'

The Duke's eyes sharpened. He had long ago come to the conclusion that there was more to the little Riccardi than met the eye. Her manner of talking about the King's mistress and prospective mistress only increased that feeling. She spoke as if she knew them personally. Yet what contact would the proud Athénaïs have had with Marietta, unless it was commercial?

'Did you practice lacemaking in Paris, Marietta?'

Marietta's concentration remained on her intricate work, her fingers never resting. 'Of course. I am a lacemaker. Wherever I go I make lace.'

'So *that's* how you know La Montespan?'

Céleste's eyes rounded. 'Did you *really* make lace for Madame de Montespan? Is it true that she is the King's new favourite and

La Valliére is heartbroken? Does she really pretend to be the Queen's friend?'

'Madame de Montespan pretends all sorts of things.'

'That's no way to speak of her,' the Duke said, toying with his snuff box. 'It would be dangerous for Elise to go to Versailles with prejudiced ideas of Madame de Montespan.'

'It would be dangerous for her to go with other ideas,' Marietta said steadily. 'The worst thing that could happen to Elise is that Athénaïs de Montespan should befriend her.'

The Duke's voice hardened. He had no *tendresse* for Athénaïs, finding her too cold and calculating, and he was grateful to Marietta for her refusal to marry his son, but it went against his honour to hear her talk in such a manner of a lady of his own class. 'Selling lace to the nobility does not give you the right to make gross assumptions of their characters, Marietta.'

She raised her eyes to his. 'Madame de Montespan came to the Riccardis for more than lace,' she said quietly.

The silence lengthened and their eyes held. The Duke de Malbré had no way of understanding what was behind her words and had more sense, in the present company, than to ask. Something in her manner sent a cold chill down his spine.

196

They would have to have a long talk tonight, away from the avid ears of Céleste.

Marietta was no idle gossip eager for any attention careless words could give her. She knew something about the great Madame de Montespan, and his sixth sense told him it was best kept to herself. Unless it could possibly affect Elise. He was suddenly quite sure that he would rather move heaven and earth than have that sweet angel contaminated by the likes of the worldly Athénaïs.

But it was her husband's duty to see to that, not his. All he could do was advise. The knowledge robbed him of his former feeling of well-being. He was living in a fool's paradise. If he had a grain of sense he would return to court immediately, not remain at Chatonnay on the pretext of waiting for a wedding he now dreaded. He poured himself a goblet of Marietta's cinnamon-flavoured wine, reflecting that the older men grew, the more foolish they became.

Céleste, seeing that the intriguing subject of Madame de Montespan was now closed, cast round in her mind for another. She found it and it was one that caught even Léon's attention.

'Did you know that the witch-hunters are in Montpellier?'

There was a gasp from behind her and Céleste smiled, well satisfied. It wasn't often that anyone took Marietta by surprise. Léon's eyes darkened.

'Who told you such idiocy?'

'Armand – and it's not idiocy. Everyone is talking about it. They are looking for a very powerful, very beautiful witch. Armand says she is Lucifer's mistress, and he has sent her to Languedoc to wreak havoc amongst us.'

'Sent her from where?' the Duke asked idly.

'From Paris.'

'So our enchantress is a French-woman?' The Duke was smiling again.

'No, of course not,' Céleste said indignantly. 'She is a foreigner, but she has vast knowledge of charms and potions and can curse you in the twinkling of an eye. That's why the witch hunters of Paris have come to hunt her down.'

Jeannette, aware of how painful the apparently harmless conversation must be to Marietta, said firmly, 'Let's have no more of witches and such nonsense. Are you visiting Elise tomorrow, Céleste?'

'Yes, and witches *aren't* nonsense,' Céleste continued, undeterred. 'This enchantress comes from a long line of witches. The Inquisitor burned her grandmother further north, and now he is searching day and night for her, before she deceives the whole of the Midi and curses us all.'

'Rubbish,' Jeannette said, standing up, her

face pale. 'Please help me up the stairs to bed, Céleste, and no more talk of witches and demons and hobgoblins.'

As she passed Marietta's chair she squeezed her shoulder, giving her a silent sign of sympathy and reassurance.

Marietta was grateful for it. What had at first only been suspicion had deepened into horrifying certainty. The witch-hunters of Montpellier were the witch-hunters of Evray. *She* was the enchantress they spoke of. *She* was their prey. She felt sick and giddy and had to steel herself from crying out in fear. This talk of cursing the good people of Languedoc was nothing but a blind to receive help from the townspeople and villagers. Any stranger would be immediately reported to them, especially if she were young and beautiful and skilled in making potions...

With trembling hands she laid her work down, and carefully avoiding Léon's eyes bade him and the Duke goodnight.

Her lips, already bruised and tender from Léon's savage love-making of the day before, began to bleed once again as she bit them in her fear. In the privacy of her room she pressed a handkerchief against her mouth, staring at the bright red spots. Blood. That was what the black-robed Inquisitor and his finely-dressed friend wanted. Her blood.

With trembling hands she undressed and slipped a soft clean nightdress over her head.

The darkness had never worried her before, now it was full of nameless horrors. She lit a candle but the small flickering flame offered no comfort; the shadows it made only increased her fear. She heard Léon wish the Duke and Raphael goodnight and heard their measured treads as they walked towards their rooms. Then silence.

She tried to sleep and failed. Montpellier was not far away. How long would it be before a careless word from Armand or Céleste or any of the villagers that she now knew, betrayed her? Should she leave now or was it already too late? Her head ached with unanswered questions.

She had to speak to Léon, but there were too many listening ears in the château. It would be impossible to have such a sensitive conversation with him without Cécile or Lili or Mathilde overhearing. She would have to speak to him tonight. Alone.

She pulled a flowered satin wrap around her shoulders and quietly opened her door. A few candles still lit the passage as she made her way past Céleste's room; past Jeannette's bedchamer and into the far wing that housed Léon's rooms. She had never been there before; her refurbishing of the château had stopped short of Léon's territory. From beneath a heavily carved door filtered a faint glimmer of light. It had to be Léon there, as disturbed and wakeful as she was herself.

Gently she turned the handle and pushed. The room was lit by candles in iron wall brackets. Through the leaded casement windows she could see the dark silhouettes of the plane trees that lined the avenue. A brass-studded coffer gleamed alongside a high-backed leather chair. Hardly daring to breathe, she closed the door behind her and walked into the room. A large curtain hung at an archway, and from behind it came the sound of movement. Tentatively she lifted it to one side, and froze.

He was half naked. The candlelight cast tawny gleams on his broad shoulders and arm-muscles. In front of him was a pitcher of water and a pewter washing bowl. The water still moved, shimmering with reflected light. Sensing her presence, he turned and only at the expression in his eyes did Marietta realise her stupidity. One did not enter a man's bedchamber late at night expecting to find him fully dressed. There could be only one reason for such a visit, especially when the lady in question wore only a nightdress and a captivating flowered satin wrap.

'Oh, I'm sorry! I didn't mean...' Her cheeks were scarlet and she let the curtain drop and rushed for the door.

He was there seconds before her, his back against it so that she was checked in her flight. 'Don't run away from me, Marietta.'

She was faced with a broad chest covered with a black pelt of curls.

'I didn't mean to catch you so unawares,' she said, unable to raise her eyes to his. Only inches separated them. In a moment she could be in his arms, forgetting pride, forgetting Elise, forgetting everything but her deep overpowering need of him.

'I came because I wanted to talk to you about the witch-hunters of Montpellier,' she said, trying to control the pounding of her heart.

'Ah. The witch-hunters in Montpellier,' Léon gazed at her through narrowed eyes. She had come to him, as she always did, not for love but for protection. For love she sought the all too-welcoming arms of Raphael.

'You need have no fear of them.'

'Thank you.' There was so much more she wanted to ask. So much more she wanted to say, but not when she could feel his breath on her cheek and smell the masculinity of him. Not when her finger-tips ached to reach out and touch the bare flesh before her.

The soft outline of her breasts showed clearly beneath the thinness of her wrap and nightdress, and he was unable to control his desire any longer. Slowly he lowered his head to hers and she turned away sharply before their lips could meet. Her nails dug hard into her palms.

'Am I so repugnant to you?' he asked bitterly. 'There was a time when I thought you spurned my advances purely because of Elise. Now I know it is because your heart is elsewhere, yet still you come to me for help and protection. It is your lover's bed-chamber you should be in, not mine.'

'I have no lover,' Marietta said tightly.

'That's not what de Malbré says.'

'I cannot help what another says. I can only tell you of myself. I have no lover.'

'Then you'll marry for money?' He laughed mirthlessly. 'Mother of God, I should have realised it long ago. You soon gave up your interest in me when you found I was betrothed, but Raphael was a different proposition, wasn't he? Rich and titled. I did well by you, Marietta, bringing you to Chatonnay. It's time you repaid me.'

This time there was no avoiding the mouth that came down on hers, hard and unyielding. And it was impossible for Marietta to resist any longer. With a whimper her arms moved up and around him, her lips meeting his passionately and without restraint. Then, all too soon, he held her away from him, breathing harshly.

'If I wanted you now I could have you for the asking, couldn't I? And not a thought of the man you are about to marry.' The expression in his eyes was worse than anything that had yet happened to her. Worse than her fear in Evray. Worse than her fear of the men in Montpellier.

'No,' she protested. 'You don't understand.'

'I understand very well.' His words cut through her like a knife. 'You're a trollop, Marietta Riccardi. An entrancing, inflaming, clever little trollop!'

'And you're a fool!' Her voice was a sob as the hand that had been buried deep in his hair scratched its way down his face. 'I would no more marry Raphael de Malbré than I would marry you!'

She ran blindly from the room, the door slamming behind her, leaving Léon alone, his fingers rising slowly to touch his bleeding cheek.

Chapter Eight

She ran headlong into Raphael, emerging from his room to retrieve a decanter of brandy to induce sleep. Her hair was dishevelled, her mouth bruised from Léon's kiss, her body showing clearly beneath the thinness of her night-clothes. Raphael took in the situation at a glance, his eyes narrowing angrily. His arm shot out and grasped her wrist, halting her headlong flight.

'Let me go! It is not what you think, Raphael.'

'It is enough. I knew you were his mistress. But now, after I have asked you to become my wife...'

'And I have refused.'

'Because of de Villeneuve?' Raphael's blue eyes were hard as agates. 'He's a man about to marry, a man who did not even protest at the thought of losing you. He does not love, nor ever will. For years Versailles has said that the Lion of Languedoc is incapable of such emotion. He is like Henri IV. He drinks. He fights. He makes love, but he does not love. Ask any one of a hundred women. Only the angelic Widow Sainte-Beuve has his heart, and even *she* won't have that when it ceases to breathe.'

Raphael's blue eyes were ferocious. He let go of Marietta abruptly, striding back into his bedchamber and seizing his sword from its scabbard.

'No! Raphel! Listen to me!' She hung on to his arm trying to restrain him, her face white with terror. 'It's not what you believe, Raphael! Truly! It has never been. I *know* Léon has never loved me.'

'And you still creep to his room at night?' Raphael asked scathingly.

'Not for lovemaking! Mother of God, if you only knew! Just now, when I would have yielded to him, he spurned me. The only overtures he has ever made to me have been those of an uncaring nobleman to the lowest of his peasants.'

'And you submitted?' Raphael felt a jealousy he had never thought possible.

Her voice broke on a sob. 'No. Only tonight. Just for a moment … and then he called me a trollop.'

'Why, if you have always refused him?'

'Because of you,' she said, 'because he believes I have accepted your proposal of marriage.'

'And you have not?'

'No.' Her eyes were filled with such pain that Raphael de Malbré's heart twisted.

'You see, I love Léon. I will always love Léon.'

Raphael's anger subsided. Even his jealousy was fading. He knew then that he had lost.

'*Ma pauvre petite!* I will cause you no more pain, I promise you. Go to your bed now. You are shivering.'

'And Léon?' A flicker of fear returned to her eyes.

Raphael permitted himself a wry smile. 'I shall not run him through with a sword, if that is what you fear. I doubt I should have accomplished such a feat even if I had attempted it. Goodnight, *ma chére.*'

He watched her walk along the shadow-filled passageway to her own room: a lonely figure with bowed shoulders. He closed his own door behind him and proceeded towards the room of his friend.

Léon was staring through the darkened panes of his window as Raphael entered. He was still not prepared for bed. His body gleamed in the candlelight, and at the sight of Léon's massive shoulders and strong arm-muscles Raphael gave a sigh of relief that he had not come to his room intent on a fight.

Léon turned to him, his face darkening. The last person he wanted to see was Raphael de Malbré. Marietta's words still rang in his ears, filled with such savagery

207

and truth that he could not help but believe them.

'I would like to speak with you, my friend,' Raphael said, sitting down easily in the brass-studded leather chair and helping himself to a glass of brandy. There were, he saw, several empty decanters on the far table. It seemed he wasn't the only one who had resorted to spirits to blur his senses.

Léon waited silently, his shoulders tense.

'It seems I cannot tempt the entrancing Marietta to become the Duchesse de Malbré after all.'

The silence continued. Raphael toyed with his glass.

'It seems her heart is elsewhere, and that it is a very loyal one. A pity that it should be treated so callously, my friend.'

Slowly Léon walked into the centre of the room and faced him.

Raphael shook his head in wonder. 'Lord of grace, but you're a fool, Léon! To marry an old man's toy like Elise when you could have Marietta for a wife. Are you mad? Elise will never be mistress of Chatonnay. It is upon Mathilde that the comfort and running of your home will fall, and as to what that comfort will be...' Raphael shrugged expressively. 'How long have we known each other? Twenty years? Twenty-two? I know what you want from life. To rear your children here, on the soil of the south. To hunt and hawk with them.

'Elise will hand her children over to a wet nurse. If she has any,' he added for good measure. 'Then they will be farmed out to aristocratic houses in Paris as are other children of your class, whose parents stay stubbornly on in the provinces. Elise is capable of nothing else. She tires after one dance. She tires too easily to ride, or to hawk, or to even play chess.'

Nearly, but not quite, he said she would tire too easily to make love. There were things which could not be said, and Raphael knew he had nearly crossed the acceptable limit. He poured himself another brandy.

'So why this constancy to Elise Sainte-Beuve when there is one who suits you so much better? One who loves you with an intensity any man would envy?'

Léon raised his hands to his throbbing temples. 'Sweet Jesus, Raphael, it had been six years! For six years I carried Elise's memory with me. She stood for everything that I cherished. Chatonnay. Languedoc. I built up a vision of our life together here…' He broke off, his face anguished, and silently Raphael handed him his brandy. 'If I had not met Marietta I would have married her.'

'And died of boredom,' his friend finished for him.

Léon smiled bitterly. 'No doubt. Already I

dread the endless hours at Lancerre, talking about fashions and other inanities. The doings of the King. Whether the Queen is aware of La Montespan's intrigue with him. Things in which I have no interest and never shall.'

'Then why marry her?'

'I shall not. I ride to Lancerre tomorrow to inform her of the fact. It will hurt her unbearably, but there is no other course of action open to me. I know now that I do not love her, that I never loved her. That it was only a dream – a mirage.'

'Then I suggest,' Raphael said, rising to his feet, 'that you inform Marietta of that fact and of another one.'

'Which is?'

'That it is her you love.'

And he let himself out of Léon's room, reflecting that his friends at court would never believe it. He, Raphael de Malbré, handing over a prize like Marietta Riccardi without so much as a fight. He wondered if he was wanting in the head, and then remembered the agony in the lustrous green eyes as they had gazed up at him and she had said, 'I love Léon. I will always love Léon.'

Perhaps this one selfless action would redeem him for the many hearts he had broken and the countless husbands he had deceived. It was a droll thought, and he smiled as he snuffed his candle and lay down in his bed. Céleste, he reflected as sleep engulfed him, was really quite a pretty girl. And it was foolish to grieve for a love one could not have.

Marietta crept into bed, emotionally exhausted. A trollop. She, Marietta Riccardi, a trollop! She buried her face in the pillow, wondering if her life would be long enough for her ever to forget the look of contempt on his face as he had thrust her from him. His behaviour had been unpardonable. Inexcusable. Why should she, a Riccardi, suffer so much because a man who was arrogant and overbearing should fail to love her?

She closed her eyes against the hurt, wondering if it wouldn't have been better if he had left her to her fate at Evray.

Léon, too, was sleepless. Raphael said Marietta loved him, but after his behaviour was it possible that she still did so? He groaned and ran his fingers through his hair. Only time would tell. He would speak to her in the morning, but that was hours away. He slipped on his linen shirt and leather jerkin and descended the stairs, quietly whistling his dogs. Then, a musket under his arm, he let himself out of the château, striding over the drawbridge into the darkness.

It was early morning before he returned. He slung two herons and six hares on to the wooden kitchen table, but Marietta, taking the first batch of wheaten loaves out of the oven, gave no indication of being aware of his presence. Her back was straight, her head held high. Her face was a little paler than usual, but otherwise there was no sign of the tears she had shed through the night.

'Thank you, Monsieur le Comte,' Cécile said, removing the bloodied game from the table to clean.

He didn't seem to hear her. He was staring at Marietta as she shaped the dough for a second batch of bread with unnecessary vigour. Cécile felt suddenly uncomfortable. Why was he staring at Marietta like that? It was a look Cécile had never seen on her master's face before. Almost pleading.

She shook herself and hurried away with the birds. The Lion of Languedoc wouldn't demean himself to plead for the favours of any woman. Not even the highest in the land. She was imagining things. Nevertheless, there was a very strange atmosphere in the kitchen and she would have had to be blind not to see the deep scratches running down his cheek. *Those* would take some explaining away to the pretty Madame Sainte-Beuve. She could not help looking over her shoulder curiously as she crossed the courtyard. The bread was taking Marietta an unconscionable long time to prepare, and it seemed to Cécile that neither of them had moved.

The bread was put aside to rise at last and Marietta marched purposefully past him to the pantry.

'Marietta, I've come to talk to you.'

'I'm busy, Monsieur le Comte.' Her voice was devoid of expression.

'Marietta, I've come to apologise.'

She poured vinegar into a flask, adding rosemary and lavender.

'Your apology is accepted, Monsieur le Comte.'

'For God's sake, stop this *Monsieur le Comte* business,' Léon said exasperatedly.'

She faced him, her head defiantly high. 'But that is who you are, Monsieur le Comte, and I, as you so clearly pointed out last night, am a trollop.' She corked the flask and walked past him to the courtyard and her waiting mare.

He resisted the urge to take her by the shoulders and shake her. After all, he deserved her contempt. She was hardly likely to fall willingly into his arms after the way he had treated her the previous evening.

'Marietta!' He strode after her, determined to make her listen, but she had already vaulted into the saddle and the sound of his mother's voice prevented him from dragging her forcibly to the ground.

He turned impatiently to Jeannette. 'Yes? What is it?'

'Céleste has accompanied Elise's steward to greet a wedding guest newly arrived in Montpellier!'

'Lord of grace! If that stupid child opens her mouth in Montpellier we'll have the witch-hunters at Chatonnay within hours! Tell Henri to give my apologies to Elise. Tell him to tell her I won't be able to see her today, that I have business in Montpellier.'

Jeannette stared at him, seeing for the first time the angry scratch-marks.

'What has happened to your face?'

'I've been hunting,' he said curtly, indicating the hares on the table.

'But that's no reason for…'

'If I want to get to Montpellier in time to stop Cécile doing any harm I'll have to hurry.' He picked up his gauntlets, drawing them on as he strode out into the courtyard and to the stables, not bothering to even change his leather jerkin for more suitable attire.

'Why so downcast?' Henri asked Jeannette as Léon mounted Saracen and clattered noisily out of the courtyard and towards the drawbridge.

'Selfish thoughts,' Jeannette said, knowing she could tell him nothing of her anxieties for Marietta's safety or for her son's happiness. 'Léon has asked that you give

214

Elise a message from him. He has had to go to Montpellier and will not be able to see her today.'

The Duke brightened, unable to conceal his pleasure at the prospect of Madame Sainte-Beuve's company without the intrusion of her husband-to-be. Jeannette wondered if she should ask him about his feelings for her future daughter-in-law, and decided against it. Life was complicated enough at the moment.

'Perhaps Marietta would like to accompany me?' Henri asked, hoping that she would not.

'Marietta has already left for the Brissacs.'

'But I thought the Brissac girl was completely recovered?' The Duke raised his eyebrows slightly.

Jeannette made a helpless motion with her hands. 'So did I, but everyone seems to be behaving strangely. Léon spent half the night out hunting and Céleste has gone to Montpellier with Elise's steward.'

'What the devil for?'

'To greet a wedding guest and escort him to Lancerre.'

'Or to see the witch-hunters,' Henri said with a laugh.

Jeannette forced a smile. 'I should think that even Céleste has more sense than that,' she said, wishing she could sound more convincing.

'Monsieur le Duc,' Elise gasped, her face brightening as Henri entered the room bearing a gift of sweetened angelica.

'I bring bad news, not good,' he said genially. 'Léon has business in Montpellier, and so will be unable to visit Lancerre to-day.'

Elise made a little sound of disappointment, and then said with childish pleasure, 'Angelica! I haven't had sweetened angelica for ages. You *are* kind.'

'If we were in Paris I would have sent you sapphires to match your eyes,' he said gallantly. 'As it is I'm like the poorest peasant. All I can offer is angelica.'

A blush rose to Elise's cheeks. 'I believe that Madame de Montespan wears sapphires,' she said shyly.

The Duke remembered Marietta's veiled hints as to her knowledge of that lady, and chastised himself for not already seeking her out and questioning her about it. He would do so tonight. It would be soon enough. For the moment all that mattered was Elise.

He turned his attention fully back to her, where it was wholeheartedly reciprocated. The conversation, as always, was firmly on Versailles, and the Duke saw no need to request Elise's dour-faced housekeeper to act as chaperone. Neither, happily, did Elise. In the Duke's company she blossomed like a flower in the warmth of the sun, her soft laughter filling the terraces and flower-filled garden. The servants looked at each other. There was no laughter to be heard when the Lion of Languedoc came visiting. Then their mistress remained tongue-tied and uncomfortable, which was a very strange state of affairs considering that he was her lover and her betrothed.

Elise and Henri continued to enjoy the peace and tranquillity of the afternoon, unaware that only miles away Marietta was facing death from the oldest enemy of man.

Angrily Marietta spurred her mare out of courtyard towards the Brissacs' cottage, unshed tears in her eyes. Damn him! Did he think all he had to do was offer an apology and she would forget his insults? Perhaps it had occurred to him that she could quite easily tell Elise of his advances. That, not remorse, was the reason for his so-called apology. Her hair streamed in the wind and she dug her heels into the mare's side, urging her faster and faster across the sun-baked earth.

She had no real need to visit Ninette. The girl was once again fit and well. Her journey had only been an excuse to leave the château, to have some time to herself for thinking things out quietly, away from

Léon's disturbing presence. If the witch-hunters were in Montpellier then her presence at Chatonnay was a danger to them all. To Jeannette: to Céleste: and to Léon. Now was the time to do what she had always known she must do eventually – leave the château that had become her home. Leave Jeannette, who was daily becoming like her own mother. And leave Léon, never to see him again.

The de Villeneuve wedding gown would never be finished. It had been a daydream of the future, not a vision. She would leave today, quietly and unobtrusively. She left the track, climbing up into the hills. Below her she could see the Montpellier road. Soon, very soon, a black-robed figure would ride that way towards Chatonnay, and when it did, she, Marietta Riccardi, would have to be far away.

She slipped from her mare's back, letting it wander freely as she sat in the shade of a giant tumble of rocks. A lizard ran across her path and she shielded her eyes against the heat haze. Surely that was Léon riding for Montpellier? Only he sat a horse with such ease and arrogance, and there were few stallions as distinctive as Saracen in Languedoc.

From nearby came a sound that drove all thoughts of the distant horseman from her mind. A sound that rooted her to the spot in a terror ages old, the unmistakable sound of a wolf.

'Blessèd Jesu,' she whispered, scrambling to her feet. 'Not that! Clothilde! Clothilde!' But the mare had sharper ears than Marietta, and was already dashing headlong down the hillside in a terrified frenzy.

Sweat broke out on Marietta's forehead. If she ran the wolf would pounce on her. If she was very still and it was not in search of food it was just possible that it would pass her by.

'Holy Mary, Mother of God,' she whispered, 'pray for us sinners now and at the hour of our death…'

There came the soft thud of a heavy body jumping to the ground, and the threatening grey form of a wolf emerged from a thicket of trees. It moved towards her, its back arched, its coat bristling. Marietta screamed and continued screaming. Her only hope of safety was to hide herself in a niche of rock that the ravening animal could not penetrate. Feverishly she sought a gap in the tumble of boulders. Only smooth stone met her clawing fingers. She could hear the panting breath; could sense the beast only yards behind her. She turned, flattening herself against the stones, senseless with terror. Her screams rang out over the deserted countryside. Deserted except for one figure and Marietta, her eyes locked with those of the deadly animal padding towards her, was not even aware of Saracen galloping furiously up the hillside in a flurry of dust and falling stones.

She was powerless to move now. Threateningly the animal approached, nearer and nearer; crouching low on its haunches, preparing to spring.

'Please Lord! No! Please Lord! Sweet Lord...' Her heart pounded, the blood drumming in her ears. Had she escaped the flames for this? To be torn limb from limb by a fiend with slavering fangs and blood-red eyes? The haunches tightened, and she closed her eyes and gave one last scream.

She never saw him appear. One minute there was nothing in the world but the wolf and herself and the next Léon was there, leaping from Saracen's back with a dagger held high in his hand. The animal turned, springing viciously towards him, and Léon leapt at it, the knife plunging into the base of its throat. They fell together, the wolf still thrashing, man and beast covered in blood. Then, after what seemed an eternity, Léon rose unsteadily to his feet and the wolf lay motionless.

'Oh, my God! Oh, Léon! Léon!' She threw herself into his arms, uncaring of the blood, uncaring of everything. 'Has he hurt you? Are you all right? Speak to me, Blessèd Jesu, please speak to me!'

He held her so close she could hardly

breathe and, still holding her prisoner, he asked, 'Am I no longer *Monsieur le Comte,* to be kept at a frigid distance?'

She raised a tortured face to his. 'How can you talk so? You know I didn't mean it.'

'I only know what you have shown me, my sweet love. Contempt and scorn.'

'No! It's you who has shown nothing but contempt. Calling me a trollop, while I … I…' She faltered, aware for the first time that she was trapped in his arms and that he showed no signs of releasing her.

'Yes?' he asked softly.

There was blood on his face and jerkin. She could feel its sticky warmth seeping into her bodice. He was hurt and bleeding, but all she could do was stay pressed close to him, her heart turning over as the dark eyes burned into hers.

'While I loved you,' she said at last.

'And I you.'

Her knees weakened and without his support she would have fallen.

'Elise?' she whispered almost inaudibly.

'Elise will be hurt, but not as much as she would have by marrying a man who does not love her.'

'Oh, Léon, do you mean it?' She could hardly breathe. Her entire life depended on his answer.

'I mean it,' he said huskily. 'The men of Evray were right, you are a witch. You bewitched me the minute I set eyes on you and it's my belief you will continue to do so until death – and beyond.' He kissed her tenderly and then with increasing passion. Her mouth answered his with a savage joy, her arms around his neck, her fingers deep in the riotous curls.

'Hell's light, what a fool I've been,' he said at last as he lifted his mouth from hers and stared down at the heart-shaped face that had haunted him waking and sleeping. 'And to have it pointed out to me by a de Malbré! Will you ever forgive me, my sweet love?'

'There is nothing to forgive,' she said, her mouth still sweet from his kisses. 'You acted as you did out of honour.'

His lips curved in a faint smile. 'Not completely. You'd make a saint forget honour,' and he kissed her again, this time with hunger and the longing of a man long starved.

Her body yielded pleasurably against his. It was as if all his strength passed into her and she knew that never again would she be afraid. 'The vision,' she said softly as his lips moved to her forehead, kissing the satin-smooth softness in a gesture of homage.

'Only witches have visions,' he said caressingly, his eyes laughing down at her.

She shook her head. 'Sometimes the good Lord gives them to those who pray.'

'And what did you pray for, sweet love?'

'For a husband who would love me so much that he would fight even a wild beast for me.'

He smiled. 'Then your prayer has been answered – and not only wild beasts but witch-hunters and snakes. You've ruined more of my tunics than have ever been ruined in battle. And brought me nearer to death.'

Horrified, she looked down at the blood that stained his clothes, noticing for the first time the rents in his shirt and jerkin.

'Oh! You *are* hurt. Why didn't you tell me?'

'Because I was too busy kissing you,' he retorted truthfully.

'Where is the blood coming from? Show me quickly.'

With a grimace of pain he tore open his shirt, revealing a chest scored by claw marks.

'Blessèd Jesu,' she whispered, her eyes widening, and then she was spurred into action, staunching the flow of blood with her hastily discarded petticoat.

'First my face, now my chest,' he said wryly.

Her eyes were anguished. 'I didn't mean to mark your face like that. Truly.'

'Or get chased by witch-hunters and wolves?'

'Of course not.' She was indignant.

'I think I would prefer to make love to you

away from the carcase of that wretched animal, and in more comfortable surroundings. Where is your horse?'

'The coward ran off.'

'She'll find her way home. Let's mount Saracen. After all, he is quite used to carrying the two of us.' And with his arm tight around her waist they walked to where Saracen waited. With a wince of pain Léon vaulted into the saddle, and Marietta swung herself up behind him, her arms around him, her head against the broadness of his back, just as it had been in their flight from Evray.

Neither of them remembered the witch-hunters in Montpellier, or Céleste gaily meeting Elise Sainte-Beuve's wedding guest and prattling artlessly about the beautiful newcomer at Chatonnay.

Chapter Nine

'Did you truly love me from the minute you set eyes on me?' she asked, her lips pressed close to the thick black curls.

'Ever since you so graciously slapped my face,' Léon affirmed, a faint smile tugging at the corners of his mouth despite his pain. 'And what of you, my sweet love? Since when did I cease to be so objectionable to you?'

She nuzzled her head closer to the glossy curls. 'You have never been objectionable to me, Léon. Never. I've loved you ever since the night at Evray when you called me an old beldame!'

Despite their predicament; the blood that was drying on her bodice and clotting on Léon's jerkin, there was a hint of laughter in her voice. She would bathe his wounds in brandy the minute they reached Chatonnay. Léon was strong; he would suffer no ill effects from his duel with the wolf. And he would be hers for ever and all eternity. The claw marks would leave scars but they would be a constant reminder of the moment their love had been acknowledged.

She sighed, and it was the sigh of a truly

happy woman. One who wanted nothing else in life but that which she held in her arms.

'And may a man ask his future wife why she loves him with such devotion?' The expression in his voice made her heart race.

'It isn't because I would be lonely without you. I had already faced up to a life for ever on my own. It isn't because I want to be a Comtesse. It isn't even love for love's sake. It is because you are in my heart and in my blood. You are part of me, Léon. You will always be part of me. I love you because I cannot help it.'

Léon's throat constricted as he covered her hands with his. They were of the same spirit: as wild and as free as the hawks they had flown together with such joy. His dream of life at Chatonnay would come true. His sons would hunt and hawk at his side, as would his wife. The love between them would be their fortress and their peace.

'I love you, Marietta Riccardi,' he said huskily, and then Saracen was walking gently over the wooden drawbridge and already Jeannette was running towards them, her eyes glazed with fear at the sight of her blood-soaked son.

'What has happened? Who has hurt you? Oh, Léon! *Léon!*' Her last cry held a familiar note of exasperation and Léon grinned, remembering it from the days of his childhood, from the days when he would return bloodied and bruised from fights with the village boys.

'It's all right, Mother, it isn't half as bad as it looks. Mere claw marks. Nothing more.'

'*Claw* marks?'

With his arm around Marietta's waist Léon walked into his home. For the first time it occurred to Jeannette that he was not holding on to Marietta for support, and that he was quite capable of walking unaided.

'A wolf,' he said negligently as the Duke and Raphael forgot their usual elegant nonchalance and broke into a run to meet him as he entered the hallway.

'Only one?' Raphael asked drily, noting the way Léon's arm rested tightly around Marietta's waist and the way her cheeks were flushed and her eyes radiant with happiness. So his sacrifice had been worthwhile. Léon had wasted no time. The little Riccardi was happy at last.

'I'm afraid so,' Léon answered with a grin. 'Perhaps a whole pack would have been more theatrical, but one was quite enough, I assure you!'

'I need hot water and bandages and brandy and the bottle of coltsfoot mixture,' Marietta was telling a wide-eyed Cécile, 'and quickly, or infection will set in.'

'Or love,' Raphael said in an undertone as Léon allowed him to give him some support as he climbed the stairs to his bedchamber.

'That set in long ago, as you well know.'

The two grinned at each other – the animosities and jealousies of the last few days forgotten. The Duke and Jeannette stared after them, appalled. Léon's arm was still tight around Marietta's waist, and there was a proprietorial air in the way she had ordered Cécile to fetch bandages and lotions – and she entered his bedchamber with him as though she were a wife.

'Blessèd Mary,' Jeannette whispered, her concern at the wolf paling into insignificance beside the new one that now beset her. 'What is to be done now?' and she picked up her skirts and hurried after them up the stairs.

The Duke's fine-featured face was hard. He had left Léon's bride-to-be only an hour ago, and where had Léon been? Not in Montpellier as he had said, but cavorting around the countryside with the red-haired chit who had already enslaved his son. He turned abruptly to the drawing-room and a glass of wine. Léon could bleed to death for all he cared. He was hurting the angelic Elise, and for that Henri would never forgive him.

The remnants of jerkin and shirt had already been eased off by Raphael and Marietta by the time Jeannette breathlessly entered the room. At the sight of her son's lacerated chest she gasped, paling so that Raphael thought she would faint.

'A chair, madame,' he said, crossing hastily to her and seating her against her will. 'There is nothing for you to do. Marietta will see to everything.'

'Yes.' Dazedly she watched the tableau in front of her as Cécile and Lili hurried in with hot water and bandages and the brandy and coltsfoot lotion that Marietta had asked for. She watched the expression in Léon's dark eyes as they rested on the heart-shaped face and concerned green eyes, the tender way in which she bathed his wounds. His hand rising to touch her cheek; her hair. It was as if no one else was in the room with them.

Jeannette's head ached. What had happened since yesterday, when Léon would scarce speak two civilised words with Marietta? Why was Raphael, so proud where his honour was concerned, displaying no anger at the open tenderness between her son and the girl he was to marry? Not tenderness, she corrected herself: love.

The wounds were bathed in brandy, washed clean, and dressed in bandages soaked in coltsfoot lotion. Léon looked hardly the worse for his bloody encounter. In fact, he looked better than he had done since he had returned home. His hand, now that Cécile and Lili had been despatched with empty bowl and bottles, tightly held Marietta's. Jeannette rallied herself.

'Would someone *please* explain to me what is going on?'

'With the greatest of pleasure.' Léon's hand tightened its hold on Marietta's. 'Marietta is to be my wife.'

Jeannette struggled for strength and understanding. 'But so is Elise,' she managed to say at last.

'No longer. I ride to Lancerre now to inform her of the fact. It wasn't Elise I wanted to marry, it was just a dream. And Elise will be happier without me.'

'And Raphael?' Helplessly she turned to her son's friend. A duel between the two of them would kill her.

'I have lost nothing, madame, since I never had it in the first place. The beautiful Marietta refused my offer of marriage when I first made it. I found the fact too incredible to believe, and so our misunderstanding. Marietta has never, at any time, agreed to become my wife, or accepted any advances I made to her.'

'I see.' Jeannette leaned weakly back in the chair. Everything was going to be all right. Léon was going to marry Marietta, Marietta who she loved. Marietta who would run Chatonnay and bear strong, healthy children. Marietta who would continue to teach the village girls lace-making and bring prosperity to Chatonnay. Marietta who loved her son wholeheartedly, with every fibre of her being, as she had loved Léon's father.

'You are not angry?' Marietta asked hesitantly, filled with sudden apprehension.

'Bless you, child,' Jeannette said, her face wreathed in smiles, 'this is the happiest day of my life.' And she crossed to the bed, embracing her warmly.

'I fear I can no longer keep you company,' Raphael said, 'I have an engagement elsewhere.'

'On the Montpellier road to meet the returning Céleste,' he could have added, but didn't. When one door closed another opened, and Céleste could play the coquette quite well when given the chance. She also has the trimmest pair of ankles he had ever seen. Perhaps if he met her on her return to Chatonnay he would be able to find out if the legs above them were also slender and delectable. The three in the room were hardly aware of his departure.

Léon swung his legs off the bed, suppressing a wince of pain. 'You shouldn't go now,' Marietta said anxiously. 'You should rest.'

'Because of a few scratches?' he asked, his smile making her heart tremble. 'I've suffered worse many times.'

'Then I'm glad that I did not know of it,

or I would have suffered also.'

Slowly he took her upturned face in his hands and kissed it. 'When I return we will be able to tell the whole world of our love. Goodbye, my sweet.'

The shirt he drew on had a drawstring of lace, the sleeves puffing out in three lavish layers, cuffed deeply in *point de France* lace. In future, Marietta thought with an inward smile, his clothes would be embellished with *point de Venise*. He looked once more every inch a Comte as he strode out of the room and down the stairs to the stables.

'I think,' Jeannette said, watching from the window as he rode away, 'that Elise will not be quite as heartbroken as Léon fears.'

'Because of the Duke?' Marietta asked.

Jeannette smiled. 'Because of the Duke,' she affirmed. 'I think we should tell him of events. I think he will want to ride to Lancerre at the earliest opportunity to comfort the now free Widow Sainte-Beuve.'

Never had Léon rode so urgently to Lancerre. He had no desire to inflict pain on Elise; she had been the first love of his life, and if that love had been built on unreality it had nevertheless been precious to him, and he still felt a deep tenderness for her. But it was nothing compared to his all-consuming love for Marietta. If he had married Elise he would have caused her deep unhappiness. Their natures were so different that he could have done nothing else no matter how hard he had tried.

The knowledge gave him courage. The day had been a long one and it was approaching dusk by the time he had galloped into the familiarity of Elise's fountain-filled courtyard. He strode towards the door and was met by a grim-faced Abbé.

'Good evening, Monseigneur.' It was a rather grand title for the grey-haired priest but it was one that gave pleasure. This time the kind face of the Abbé did not soften. He raised his hand, barring Léon's entrance. Immediately Léon halted, his stomach muscles tight.

'What is it? Is something wrong?'

'Madame Sainte-Beuve has been taken sick, less than an hour ago. Your friend, the Duke de Malbré, visited her and after he left she complained of tiredness and headaches. Now she has a fever and is delirious.'

'Like Ninette Brissac?'

The Abbé nodded. 'And many more these last few months, who have not recovered as Ninette did.'

'Let me go to her.'

'And catch the sickness?'

Léon gave him a look of scorn and mounted the stairs to Elise's room two at a time. The frightened housekeeper gave him entry, and the sight of the tossing, semi-conscious Elise was enough for Léon to see the seriousness of the situation. 'Stay with her,' he said curtly. 'I will be back with Madamoiselle Riccardi.'

The Abbé was waiting for him by his horse. 'I have given her a blessing, but...' He shrugged expressively.

'Mademoiselle Riccardi saved Ninette Brissac. She can also save Elise.'

Léon was already back in the saddle, cursing his injured chest that slowed down his movements.

The Abbé shrugged again. If his blessing did not cure Elise what could the Riccardi girl do? Ninette Brissac had obviously not been as sick as the other girls – the girls who had died. 'The wedding guest!' he shouted after Léon. 'What of the wedding guest?'

Léon wheeled Saracen around, staring at him, transfixed. The little Abbé hurried forward.

'There is a cousin already in Montpellier. He will have to be told. There can be no wedding now, my son, not for a long time. And Lancerre should have no visitors until Madame Sainte-Beuve recovers.'

'No.' Léon's mouth was tight. He spurred Saracen, galloping as if into battle, down the dusty road towards Chatonnay. Lord of grace, but he hadn't given a thought to Céleste and Montpellier! Anything could have happened. Already the witch-hunters could be on their way for Marietta.

Saracen, sensing his master's urgency, strained himself to the limit, flanks glistening with sweat as he skidded to a stop outside his stable and Léon leapt to the ground, rushing headlong past a startled Mathilde, calling for Jeannette and Marietta at the top of his voice.

'What on earth...' Jeannette began, as she and Marietta hurtled from their rooms.

'Céleste! Has she returned?'

Jeannette gasped, her hand to her mouth. So much had happened; Léon's injuries, his declaration of love for Marietta. It had completely cast from her mind Céleste's presence in Montpellier and the danger it could bring.

'No...'

The expression on his face frightened Marietta, and she did not understand his anxiety as to Céleste's whereabouts. 'Elise?' she asked. 'Did you tell Elise?'

The eyes that held hers were grim. 'I could not. Elise is sick with fever, and if the Abbé is to be believed, close to death.'

Marietta said nothing; simply turned and began to run towards the pantry where her medicines were kept.

'Perhaps Lancerre is the best place for Marietta at present,' Léon said to his mother, his mind racing. 'She will nurse Elise. No one on earth could prevent her from doing so, even if they tried. Meanwhile, I will ride for Montpellier and Céleste.'

Jeannette licked dry lips. 'And if Céleste has spoken thoughtlessly?'

'Then the world will be shorter of witch-hunters, for I swear before God I'll kill every last one of them before they even so much set eyes on Marietta again!'

As he spoke he buckled his sword. Jeannette felt fear rise in her like a tide and tried to subdue it. Léon was no boy. He was a man, a soldier, the warrior of Louis' forces. The legendary Lion of Languedoc. She was behaving faintheartedly. She struggled to smile.

'God go with you,' she said.

He marched past her, drawing on his gauntlet. 'Tell Marietta what has happened and why I have left. She has the courage to understand. Tell her to stay at Lancerre until I come for her.'

Then he was gone, this time riding a fresh horse, the noise of its hooves bringing Marietta running into the yard in bewilderment.

'He has ridden for Montpellier,' Jeannette said, hurrying towards her. 'Céleste left early this morning to greet one of Elise's wedding guests, and Léon is afraid that she will chatter and be overheard. He was on his way there when you were attacked by the wolf.'

'I see.' Marietta's eyes were anguished, not with fear for herself but for Léon. She knew to what extent he would go to protect her.

'He told me to tell you to stay at Lancerre. Not even a witch-hunter will visit if they know there is sickness there.'

'If Elise is as sick as Ninette was, I have no other choice, but to stay with her,' Marietta said quietly. She had all she needed in her basket. She felt suddenly tired, emotionally drained. Why, oh why, did Elise have to fall sick at this precise moment?

She lifted her head. Elise *was* sick and only she, Marietta, could save her. Summoning all her strength, she walked out to where a horse waited, already saddled by the beaming Armand. Kitchen gossip had already seen to it that he knew who his future mistress was to be.

'Why so glum?' he asked, as for once Marietta allowed herself to be helped into the saddle. 'Madame Sainte-Beuve will recover, just as Ninette did.'

Marietta smiled weakly. 'I pray so, Armand.'

It seemed to take for ever to reach Lancerre, and all the way Marietta's thoughts were with Léon. Céleste had been in Montpellier for the whole of the day. There had been plenty of time for her to have chattered about Marietta's presence at Chatonnay, and if the ears of the black-robed Inquisitor should hear, or the bejewelled young man who had visited her grandmother, then there would be no future happiness with Léon. She had had plenty of time to think these last few days as she had sewed Elise's wedding gown, and now at last she knew why she was being hunted down, why her grandmother had been burned. Against such an enemy even Léon's courage would be powerless.

At last the Sainte-Beuve home, almost covered in moss and ivy, showed ahead of her. The servants greeted her with relief. They had heard of Ninette Brissac's recovery, and if this red-haired stranger could do the same for their mistress, then she would be doubly welcome. Marietta walked quickly through the rooms towards the staircase. The walls were covered with Bergamot tapestries, the Spanish leather chairs ornately gilded, heavy curtains of rich velvet at the windows. Elise enjoyed luxury. She would be happier with the Duke at Versailles than she would ever have been at Chatonnay with Léon.

'I would like bowls of lukewarm water,' Marietta said authoritatively to the house-keeper. 'Nothing else.'

While the housekeeper hurried away to do her bidding, Marietta crossed to Elise's bedside and, holding her as tenderly as she would a child, poured the carefully prepared medicine down her throat. Elise protested feverishly, trying to turn her head away, her eyes glazed and showing no recognition of Marietta.

Marietta's hold tightened. She pressed Elise's head against her breast, holding it tightly until she had protestingly swallowed a sufficient amount of the mixture. Then the housekeeper was back with the water and at Marietta's nod of dismissal, scurried away. Prayer was the only saving from the fever, and the housekeeper meant to pray fervently; not for her mistress but for herself. She didn't want to go the way of Solange Agoult, who had died only weeks ago after suffering the same symptoms as Madame Sainte-Beuve.

Alternately, Marietta sponged Elise's fevered body and gave her the medicine. The hours passed, and still Elise did not recognise her. She did not even know that she was in her own bed and at Lancerre.

'The Queen!' she cried again and again as she flung the sheets off her fevered body. 'The Queen wants me! I'm to be a lady-in-waiting. I must go now! Immediately! The Queen awaits!'

With tireless patience Marietta continued to sponge her with a constant supply of lukewarm water, press the bottle of medicine to her lips, waiting for any sign that the fever was about to break. It did not.

By dawn Elise was worse, tearing at her nightdress, the hair that usually glistened in such pretty ringlets now damp and dishevelled.

Dawn broke, and still Marietta had not slept and still Elise raved about Versailles. About her position there; her carriages; her jewels. Not once in her delirium did she call Léon's name.

The sun rose and Marietta felt faint and dizzy. She wanted sleep; a rest. Yet she could not while Elise hovered between life and death. Through the closed door the housekeeper told her that the Abbé was downstairs, and that the Duke of Malbré had arrived. But there was no news of Léon. Was he still in Montpellier? Or Chatonnay? Or – Marietta's heart seemed voluntarily to cease to beat – was he dead? Killed, acting in her defence against an evil that he knew nothing of?

'Maurice! Cousin Maurice!'

The name roused Marietta. Who was Maurice? She wiped Elise's sweating brow with a sponge soaked in camomile.

'Cousin Maurice says my position is at court! He will take me there! To the Queen as a lady-in-waiting. Oh, where is Maurice?'

She buried her head in the pillow in a frenzy, and Marietta breathed an almost imperceptible sigh of relief. No longer did Elise believe herself to be at Versailles. She knew she was still waiting to go. No doubt Maurice was the wedding guest already in Montpellier. She took Elise's hand.

'The Duke is here,' she said. 'He is most anxious for your health, Elise.'

The restless body stilled and then the wild blue eyes sought the door and she cried out. 'Léon. Is Léon here?'

'No, but he will be, Elise. He will come.'

The very sound of his name seemed to cause the fever to return in full strength. *'Léon Léon!'* Elise screamed, unable to bear the knowledge of her marriage to that masterful, frightening creature, the Lion of Languedoc.

Marietta's hand trembled as she reached out for the medicine. If Elise loved Léon so desperately, how could he possibly tell her he no longer wished to marry her when she was ill and weak? Drink this,' she said with an anguished heart, and for the first time the medicine was drunk voluntarily.

Elise fell back against the pillows, her face white, dark circles beneath her eyes. The hands that had clutched at the sheets continually through the night were now still. Marietta rose and opened the door. In the hallway below stood a taut-faced Henri and a nervous-looking housekeeper.

'Warm milk and honey,' she said. 'The fever has broken.'

The Duke de Malbré, a man used to

241

concealing his emotions in even the most trying of circumstances, mopped his brow. 'Praise God,' he said fervently. 'Praise God and all the holy angels,' and he clutched at his ebony-topped cane to prevent his knees from buckling with sheer relief.

With infinite patience Marietta spooned Elise the unwelcome goat's milk and honey, knowing that she needed sustenance if she was to recover her strength. Then Elise's eyes closed in natural sleep and Marietta sat on the floor at her bedside, Elise's hysterical cries for Léon ringing in her ears.

For the rest of the day and the following night Marietta stayed alone with Elise, giving her medicine every two hours, feeding her with the milk and honey. Léon had arrived and waited downstairs with the loyal Duke. Marietta had shed silent tears as she offered a prayer of gratitude at his safe return, but she could show no joy at his presence. Not after Elise's tortured cries for him. She had thought that the mention of the Duke's presence would bring Elise comfort, but it had been Léon's name that she had screamed, her eyes transfixed on the door. A problem that had seemed simple only a day ago now seemed insuperable.

It was dusk on the second day when she finally left the room. She swayed visibly at the top of the stairs and Léon mounted them two at a time, catching hold of her. More than anything in the world Marietta wanted to stay there, close to that strong chest, secure in loving arms. She could not. Not with Elise only yards away and the Abbé watching them with curious eyes. She withdrew herself from his embrace and said quietly, 'She is weak and will be for a long time. She does not have Ninette Brissac's natural strength. But she will live.'

'Thanks to you.' The gold-flecked eyes were so full of love and gratitude that Marietta felt she would drown in their depths.

'Come.' Despite the watching eyes of the priest, his arm encircled her waist. 'You need rest and food. Let me take you back to Chatonnay.'

She shook her head. 'You must see Elise. She cried out for you, Léon. In a voice of such pain!' Tears choked her.

Léon's brow furrowed. 'I will not speak to Elise of our marriage yet, if that is what you fear.'

'No.' She shook her head vainly. 'I fear you will never be able to speak of it to her,' and she freed herself from his hold and hurried on down the stairs to where Henri and the Abbé waited.

Léon paused, wanting to go after her, to reassure her, but the sharp eyes of the priest were watching his every movement and he turned instead to Elise's door.

'Elise?' Her eyes remained closed. He stood helplessly by the bed and then, as she showed no sign of awakening, he left the room. As the door closed behind him two tears slid from Elise's closed lids and down her cheeks. Where was Henri? Why didn't he come to her? She wanted his understanding presence, his gossip of Versailles.

'She's asleep,' Léon said as the Abbé raised surprised brows at his sudden departure. 'I will escort Mademoiselle Riccardi back to Chatonnay. She is exhausted.'

In the presence of the disapproving Abbé, Henri reluctantly rose to his feet.

'And I will accompany you.'

He turned to the housekeeper. 'Tell Madame Sainte-Beuve, should she wake, that I will be back in the morning.'

His face was tired and drawn and it occurred to Marietta that he had been at Lancerre ever since she had first seen him in the hallway.

Wearily the three of them mounted their horses and cantered out into the darkness of Lancerre's deserted streets. There was nothing that any of them could say in each other's company. Léon wanted to tell Marietta that no power on earth would prevent him from marrying her, but could not with Henri at his side. Marietta was filled with a terrible apprehension that Elise's future health would make any such marriage impossible, and Henri had thoughts only for a child-like figure, sick and ill and in no condition to accept his proposal of marriage.

They were not the only ones who had had little sleep. A wan-faced Jeannette waited for them, an anxious Céleste at her side.

'The fever broke two hours ago,' Léon said briefly and though Céleste avoided his eyes it was obvious to Marietta that nothing terrible had happened in Montpellier. It could not have, or Léon would have found some way of telling her and Céleste would not be waiting to meet them.

'Thank the Lord,' Jeannette said with heartfelt relief, and then, seeing Marietta's pale face, 'To bed with you at once. Céleste, help me assist Marietta up the stairs. She scarce has the strength to stand.'

'Allow me,' Léon said, and Marietta was swept up unprotestingly in strong arms, and despite all her tiredness at his touch a fire leaped within her. Léon! How could she live without Léon?

He lay her on the bed, and her last waking memory was of his lips on her forehead as he covered her, fully dressed, with the bed-sheets. Jeannette stood at the door, a nightdress in her hands, but he motioned her away.

'She is already fast asleep. Let her be till morning.'

Henri had already made his way exhaustedly to his room and Léon escorted his mother to hers.

'What days,' she said, leaning heavily against him. 'Is it all at an end now? No more witch-hunters? No more fears for Elise's life?'

'The witch-hunters are still in Montpellier, and we must be on our guard until they leave, but at least Céleste spoke to no one but the devastating Maurice, who seems to have quite turned her head. As for Elise, thanks to Marietta, she will live, but Marietta says she will be weak for a long time. It may be days, weeks even, before I can tell her that I no longer wish to marry her,' and he kissed her goodnight and went restlessly to his own room.

Marietta was awoken by an excited Céleste, bouncing up and down on the bed.

'Oh *do* wake up, Marietta. I've so much to tell you!'

Marietta blinked bewilderedly, expecting to see Elise nearby. Then she remembered and a smile touched her lips as she saw she was still fully clothed. Léon had carried her to her bed. She had gone to sleep with Léon's kiss on her brow.

She sat up, arranging her pillows more comfortably as Céleste said, 'I'm *so* glad Elise is better and I *know* you must have been very tired, but it's not fair of Aunt Jeannette to tell me not to wake you when it's after nine and I've no one else to talk with!'

'And what is it you want to talk about?' Marietta asked, reflecting that if it was well after nine she would have to bathe and change in a hurry, for Elise would be needing her.

'Yesterday.' Céleste's face glowed. 'Do you know that now I have *two* suitors? Raphael *and* Maurice.'

Raphael, Marietta thought, suppressing a smile, had not taken long to recover from unrequited love. 'Who is Maurice?' she asked as Céleste settled herself more comfortably and with very little regard for Marietta's feet.

'Maurice is Elise's cousin and a Marquis. I rode with Elise's valet yesterday to meet him and accompany him back to Lancerre but he had business in Montpellier and so must stay there for a few more days, which is just as well as Elise is now sick. You don't think he will return to Paris now that the wedding is to be postponed, do you?' Her eyes lost their sparkle. 'Oh, I couldn't *bear* that.'

So no one had yet told Céleste that the wedding was no longer to take place. It was still only a postponement. Marietta felt a deep-seated fear take hold of her. 'If he does he will return,' she said with an attempt at reassurance.

'But it might not be for *ages*. I think I will ask Aunt Jeannette if he can stay here, at Chatonnay.' She clapped her hands delightedly. 'To be sought after by two men under the same roof! Do you think they will become jealous and maybe fight a duel over me?'

'I should hope not,' Marietta answered chastisingly. 'That way one of them would be hurt and might possibly die and I thought you cared for them both?'

'Oh, I do.' Céleste's face, still soft with the childhood she had scarce left behind, was ecstatic. 'Raphael is so ... sophisticated. I must confess I thought he was more interested in you, Marietta, but he told me yesterday when he rode to meet me, that he was simply trying to arouse my interest by making me jealous. Can you imagine such folly? He said the tenderest things to me.' She blushed. 'He even took the liberty of kissing my foot, saying it was the daintiest he had ever seen, and then Léon came and spoiled everything.'

Her face darkened. 'Really, Cousin Léon is not a *bit* charming at times. He wanted to know where I had been, who I had spoken to. He wasn't even civil to Raphael. Only when the steward told him that we had spoken to no one but Elise's cousin did he recover any semblance of manners.'

'And is the cousin as handsome as Raphael?' Marietta asked, glad that this sudden attention had banished Céleste's sulks.

'Oh, he is divine! I think he is even richer than the de Malbrés, for his hands were covered in rings. I have never seen a diamond so huge as the one on his forefinger. Perhaps it is the one he will give to his bride-to-be!' She hugged herself. 'Duchess de Malbré or a Marchioness? I wonder what it shall be?'

Marietta smiled indulgently as she swung her legs from the bed and began to take off her crumpled gown.

'You aren't *too* disappointed about Raphael not loving you, are you?' Céleste asked as Marietta washed and then dressed in fresh clothes. 'I would understand if you are, because he is so extremely eligible and so elegant. His buttonholes yesterday were inches thick with gold thread, and I am sure the perfume he was wearing must have cost hundreds of *livres.*'

'It is a disappointment I think I can recover from,' Marietta returned gravely.

'Oh, I *am* glad. I would hate to hurt you. So now we can continue to be friends even though Raphael treated you shamefully in pretending to love you when really he was besotted by me.' She twirled in front of the mirror in a gown of brocade with a flowered silver design. 'Do you think this dress becomes me? Do you think Aunt Jeannette will allow Maurice to stay here? Do you think...?'

'Later. I must go to Elise.'

Céleste paused in front of the mirror and patted her curls. 'Cousin Léon and the Duke are waiting to speak to you in Léon's study. I quite forgot to tell you. Aunt Jeannette said that when you woke I was to send you there immediately.'

Marietta felt an all too familiar tightening of her stomach muscles. What could Léon want to say to her that he needed Henri there as witness? Had more happened in Montpellier than Céleste was aware of? Or had a night's sleep and reflection brought him to a different decision about Elise, and was he not man enough to tell her on his own? She dismissed the idea as soon as it entered her head. Not that he might have second thoughts about breaking off his betrothal to Elise, but that he would need anyone for moral support if he did so. Léon was frightened of nothing and no one.

She took a deep, steadying breath, knocked on the door and entered.

Céleste sat down on the bed in a pet. She hadn't had the chance to tell Marietta half her news: of the excitement in Montpellier that Maurice had aroused. For the Sainte-Beuve wedding was not the only reason for Maurice's presence in Languedoc. He had been sent from Paris to find the She-Devil, the witch who was about to wreak havoc in the South, so beautiful she was reputed to be Lucifer's mistress. Maurice was offering hundreds of *livres* for any information that would lead to her capture, and as he had come from Paris it could only mean that the King himself had given him his charge. And if Maurice was so close to the King...

Céleste shivered with delight. Why, perhaps if the King saw her even *he* would fall in love with her and she might follow in the footsteps of La Vallière and Madame de Montespan!

Raphael waited for her in the orchard and unknown to Léon or her aunt, Maurice also awaited her later in the day at a secret rendezvous. He had been so interested in her, listening to her every word; he, a man who consorted with the great Sun King himself! Céleste thought she would die of happiness.

She would have to be careful if she was to leave the Château without attracting attention, and she would also have to be careful not to allow his interest to stray to Marietta. He had already shown an uncommon curiosity about the red-haired girl Léon had brought back with him to Chatonnay.

But that was only to be expected. Everyone was curious about Marietta and if Maurice's interest were sincere he would have to be sure of the family he was marrying into. She pulled her gown lower to expose more of her bosom, bit her lips to redden them, and left the room, intent on meeting the first of her lovers in the orchard.

Chapter Ten

One glance at Léon's face was enough to set aside all Marietta's fears. His eyes held only love.

'Henri wishes to speak to you about Madame de Montespan. He wants to know what you meant telling him that the lady came to the Riccardis for more than lace, and to tell the truth, sweet love, so do I.'

He had crossed the room to her and now held her clasped hands against his chest. She looked up into his face. That olive-skinned face that could be so frightening in anger and so tender in love. He had risked his life by going to Montpellier and he had not known why. Now was the time to tell him.

The Duke waited patiently as Marietta gently freed herself from Léon's hold and walked slowly across to the window. Then without looking at either of them, staring out over the moat and the vine-filled plain beyond, she began:

'Madame de Montespan has always wanted to be the King's mistress. For years she flaunted herself in front of him but the King had no eyes for anyone but Louise de la Vallière. She decked herself with jewels and the richest of clothes. My grandmother made her the most superb ball dress ever seen at Versailles, and it was when wearing that dress that she finally caught the King's attention.

'There had always been rumours about my grandmother's powers. Her healing medicines had never been known to fail and some whispered she was a witch.' Marietta smiled bleakly. 'If she was, then she was a white witch, for she never did anything but good. Madame de Montespan began to come to her for beautifying lotions and creams as well as lace. By then she had won the King's heart, but Kings' hearts are fickle things, as Madame de Montespan well had cause to know.

'When she was heavy with the King's child she came to my grandmother for a love potion, something to slip in the King's wine and enflame him with desire for her and her alone. My grandmother told her that men's hearts could not be won like that and Madame de Montespan flew into a rage. At last my grandmother gave her what she asked for. It held nothing harmful – it was an aphrodisiac that was known in the days of ancient Egypt.'

She turned, her eyes holding Léon's, a faint smile in them. 'She never gave me the recipe for it, so have no fear that your own heart has been won away by stealth.'

'My own heart was lost before I ever drank or ate with you,' Léon said, and at the mere sound of his voice her heart turned over with longing for him.

'The aphrodisiac was for men who had lost their ability to love and that did not apply to the King. It had no power to hold a man's love to any one woman. Indeed, it only served to make him lustier than ever, and with one of Madame de Montespan's own maids. Madame de Montespan's fury knew no bounds. She came to my grandmother demanding that she give her a potion that she might hold the King's love for herself alone, and become Queen of France.'

There was an audible gasp from the Duke, who was watching Marietta fixedly, his face growing grimmer by the minute.

'My grandmother said there was no such potion, and then Madame de Montespan said that what the witch on the rue Beauregarde could do, surely my grandmother could do?'

'And what was that?' the Duke asked.

'To call on the powers of darkness. La Voisin is the most evil woman in France. In that house on the rue Beauregarde black masses are said over the naked bodies of some of the highest born ladies in France. The blood of new-born babes shed so that these women may attain their hearts' desires, and Athénaïs de Montespan desired the King.'

'Mother of God, do you know what you are saying?' the Duke asked, his face ashen with horror.

'Yes.' Marietta's voice was calm and composed. 'I've had plenty of time to think about it, and to wonder why my grandmother should have been hunted down and burnt so mercilessly. I thought it was because she had refused to part with her secrets of protection from poison, but I was wrong. The man who came asking for that secret was from La Montespan.'

'Protection from poison?' Henri's voice changed from horror to incredulity.

'Arsenic taken daily in minute doses will build up protection, and a large dose given by a poisoner will not have the desired effect.'

'I see,' Henri mopped his brow. 'One would have to have a lot of faith to venture on such a method of protection.'

'One has always to have faith,' Marietta replied, 'and Athénaïs de Montespan's faith is in La Voisin. My grandmother told me that the potions La Voisin was giving her were dangerous. That in trying to keep the King's love by such methods she was putting his life in danger.'

'He must be told! Immediately!' The Duke

was on his feet, his face as white as his cascading lace jabot.

'And be executed for treason in the Plâce de la Grève?' Marietta asked quietly.

'It is La Voisin and Madame de Montespan who will suffer that death!'

'No. Madame de Montespan is the King's mistress. She has given him one child and is carrying another. The King will not listen to you if you try and tell him of her visits to La Voisin. What proof have we? Only my grandmother could have testified of her requests for love philtres, and her determination to go elsewhere when refused them. Only my grandmother knew what La Voisin told her. And myself. And that is why I am being branded a witch and hunted.'

'You!' Henri's senses reeled.

'Yes, that is how Léon found me, fleeing the witch-hunters who burnt my grandmother. That is why they are now in Montpellier searching for me. They are sent from La Montespan, for she must have me silenced. There is no way I could tell the King of her association with La Voisin and be believed, but Athénaïs de Montespan is not a lady to take chances. She will have me killed and then her dark secrets will be safe.'

'Is this true?' Henri turned to Léon.

Léon nodded, his well-shaped lips in a hard line, black brows furrowed.

'Yes, and Marietta is right. The King would never believe us, not without more evidence than we now have.'

'Then he'll get it!' Henri said, his aquiline nose pinched white with fury. 'If it takes me years, he'll get it!'

'Amen to that, but for the moment we have the witch-hunters in Montpellier to contend with.'

'Not hunters. Hunter,' Henri corrected. 'There is only one.'

Marietta remembered the black-robed figure with the fanatical eyes and shivered. One was quite enough.

'The safest place for Marietta at the moment is Lancerre,' Léon said decisively. 'Then we will ride together for Montpellier, Henri.'

'Elise!' Marietta raised a hand to her mouth. 'It is nearly noon! She will be needing medicine quickly if she is to continue her recovery.'

'Then get it and let's ride with all speed. The sooner this day's business is dealt with, the better.'

As Marietta ran out of the room towards the kitchen and her basket, hastily scooping a fresh bottle of medicine from the pantry shelf, Léon and Henri buckled their swords. 'Where's Raphael?' Léon asked, a dagger going down the top of one of his leather boots.

'Courting Céleste, but the Devil knows where.'

'Find him and tell him we have more urgent matters to attend to than love-making,' Léon said grimly. 'I'll join you the minute I return from Lancerre. By tonight Marietta should be safe.'

He strode from the room, catching Marietta up in the courtyard. For a fleeting second he held her hands tight, his eyes burning into hers. 'Today there'll be no time for words of love, Marietta, but there is no need for them. You have my heart. That will suffice.'

And then he swung easily into Saracen's saddle and Marietta galloped after him on her mare, her basket over her arm, her mind in tumult. Killing the witch-hunter would not save her; La Montespan would send another, and men to murder Léon and any who helped him. Because of her both men would be riding to their deaths, and there was nothing that she could do to prevent it.

The Abbé was waiting for them, and there was no chance for last words. No opportunity for even another brief touch of the hands. He kissed her with his eyes, leaving her weak with fear and desire.

The Abbé hurried forward protestingly as Léon wheeled Saracen around, showing no sign of dismounting.

'One moment, my son. I must speak to you.'

'Not now, Monseigneur.'

'Now.' The little priest's eyes were like pinpricks, and with difficulty Léon suppressed his impatience.

'I can only give you five minutes of my time. I have urgent business to attend to.'

'As I have, my son,' the Abbé said gravely, leading Léon into the house.

Marietta was already at the top of the stairs, hurrying to Elise's bedchamber. She felt a wave of relief at opening the door and seeing Elise's maid carefully brushing her hair. If Elise had thoughts of her appearance she was truly regaining her health. Her delay had not caused a relapse.

'How good and kind you are,' Elise said, dismissing her maid and taking hold of Marietta's hand. 'My housekeeper has told me how you nursed me day and night unceasingly. I owe you my life.'

'Nonsense,' Marietta said with a smile. 'You owe me nothing but to recover your strength in the fastest time possible.'

'I fear it will be a long time,' Elise returned, leaning against her pillow, her skin almost waxen. 'I have scarce strength to raise my hand.'

'Then you must eat.' Elise shuddered and Marietta added, 'Milk and honey for two days and then some eggs lightly boiled and perhaps the breast of a chicken. You must force yourself, Elise, or you will never leave your bed.'

Elise had no desire to do so. Léon could not expect so much of her if she was confined to bed. There could be no question of tiring walks or, even worse, hawking and hunting. Bed was a welcome refuge, and one Elise intended staying in for as long as possible.

'Léon only left last night after the fever broke,' Marietta said. 'He will be here to see you shortly.'

The prospect made Elise's lower lip tremble. She wasn't strong enough to cope with Léon's demanding presence. Marietta, misunderstanding and thinking that Elise was suppressing tears of disappointment, turned away quickly, her heart tightening. Elise was so helpless! Little more than a child. How would she bear the blow they were about to deliver to her? She poured medicine and Elise took it dutifully, shuddering with distaste.

Marietta looked for a drinking glass and failed to find one.

'My maid took glass and pitcher to refill and has not returned with them,' Elise said piteously, screwing her eyes against the unpleasant taste in her mouth.

'Then I will get them,' Marietta said, 'and bring some blackcurrant juice for you next

261

time I come.'

The house was quiet as she descended the stairs, the housekeeper for once forgetting her position and joining the other servants to discuss their mistress' miraculous recovery of health. From behind the closed door the Abbé's voice came clearly.

'What you are telling me is monstrous.'

'Not monstrous.' Léon's voice was tired but firm. 'It would be monstrous for me to marry Madame Sainte-Beuve whilst I love another.'

'Whilst you *think* you love another,' the little priest corrected angrily. 'You have known and loved Madame Sainte-Beuve for six years, my son. For six years she has lived on the promise you made to her, that one day you would return. Why, the story is told far and wide! Your love for each other is becoming a legend as the stories told by the troubadours of Toulouse. And you would shame her, humiliate her, break her heart? A lady who has done nothing to hurt you or arouse such treatment? A lady so gentle and kind that even her servants call her saint? To disown such an obligation to slake a brief lust would bring you nothing but unhappiness and disfavour in the eyes of our most gracious Lord. Madame Sainte-Beuve has never enjoyed good health. Now she is weak beyond all belief and will continue to be so. She needs your care, your protection. The love that you solemnly promised her.'

Marietta could bear no more. Instead of entering the kitchen for the glass and water she walked slowly outside into the sunlight. The little Abbé was right. She and Léon could never find happiness knowing that Elise was only miles away, ill and alone and broken-hearted.

There had been a moment, when she had so rapturously accepted Léon's declaration of love, that she had believed Elise would find consolation with the adoring Duke. Elise's fevered cries had robbed her of that hope. Her happiness lay with Léon. She had waited for him six long years and Léon had tenderness for her. Without her presence perhaps it would develop into love. There was still time for her to return to Chatonnay before Léon, and to tell the Duke of her decision to leave. Then not only would Elise's happiness be secured, but neither man would risk death by riding to Montpellier to kill the witch-hunter.

Quietly she led her mare away from the house, not urging her to a gallop until they were too distant to be heard by either Léon or the Abbé. She had made the right decision, and the knowledge gave her nothing but pain. Not to see Léon again. Nor to hear his voice, feel his touch, seemed a thing too terrible to be true. Yet it had to be so. There was no other way.

The Duke, already mounted and awaiting Léon's arrival, stared at her in astonishment. 'Where is Léon?' and then, with sudden dread, 'Elise? Has anything happened to Elise?'

'Elise is well, though weak,' Marietta answered, slipping from her mare. 'I want you to do something for me, Henri. I want you to tell Léon goodbye for me.'

'Goodbye?' He stared at her incredulously.

'Yes. My reasons are my own and are sound. I have just one more task to complete before I leave, and I must hurry if I am to accomplish it before Léon returns.'

There was a determination about her that brooked no argument.

He stared after her speechlessly as she disappeared into the château. What the deuce had happened at Lancerre? And where the devil was Léon?

Marietta slipped quietly upstairs to her room. The bodice of the gown was complete. Tenderly, and with unshed tears glistening on her lashes she picked it up and the yards of heavy silk satin laid by for just such an occasion. Elise's maid would soon be able to fashion a skirt and attach the exquisite lace to make the wedding dress Elise so desired.

Henri blinked uncomprehendingly as she emerged carrying nothing but her lace and some yards of silk. No food, no wine, no provisions of any kind. She mounted her mare and turned to give him a final goodbye.

'Tell the King, if Léon refuses to return to Versailles, that he is of more service to him here, where there is so much unrest. A loyal man, able to summon a regiment at will, is of far more worth to him in Languedoc than in Versailles. The King is a man of sense. He will see the truth of the reasoning. And Henri...' Her voice was unsteady. 'Tell Léon I left him not because I did not love him, but because I loved him too well.' And then she turned her back on him, on the château, on everything that was life and breath to her and rode away, across the drawbridge and down the avenue of plane trees.

She crossed the Lancerre road, climbing up the hillside, reining in Clothilde beneath a gnarled fig tree. Then, steadfastly, she watched the shimmering road below her. She had not long to wait. In a cloud of dust Léon rode Saracen recklessly towards Chatonnay.

'Goodbye, sweet love,' she whispered, and then she dug her spurs in and rode cross-country for Lancerre. A strange horse, richly saddled, stood solitarily in the courtyard, but there was no sign of the Abbé as she breathlessly dismounted.

Carrying her precious gift she ran up the stairs and entered Elise's room. She lay asleep, her hair framing her face in a golden halo. Very carefully Marietta laid her offering at the foot of the bed. She had given all that she could and Léon would understand. Every time he saw the gown worn by his daughters and granddaughters he would remember her and the few brief hours of happiness that they had shared. Softly she tiptoed from the room and walked to the head of the stairs.

Maurice's little interlude with Céleste had told him all he wanted to know. The wench that he sought was the guest of the Lion of Languedoc, and he knew enough of that gentleman's reputation to know he could in no way publicly lay hands on her and proclaim her a witch. To do so would be to cause his own death. He would have to take her far away from the south, far away from the reach of Louis' hot-blooded warrior.

But where? Léon was master for miles around. Word of a burning in Toulouse, Narbonne, even Nîmes would soon reach his ears. It would have to be somewhere further than that. He would have to take the Riccardi wench where the Lion would never dream of looking.

The answer was so simple that he laughed softly to himself as he rode to Lancerre. Evray. He would take her back to Evray. There would be no disputing she was a witch there; the whole population already believed so. He had asked if he could meet Mademoiselle Riccardi and Céleste had guilelessly told him that he could not today – she would be at Lancerre, tending his sick relative. It seemed that most of her days were spent there. Maurice was in no hurry to see his cousin by marriage, but he was in a hurry to see the girl who nursed her.

Only the luck of the gods had prevented him from riding headlong into Léon. He had seen the swirl of dust in the distance, and prompted by a sixth sense hastily urged his horse off the road and to the cover of some fig trees. It had been the Lion all right. They had never met, but no one else would ride a horse with such skill and speed, or look so frighteningly menacing.

Maurice waited until he had disappeared before venturing from his hiding-place. The man was a fighter. It showed in every line of his taut, muscled body. He was certainly an adversary he had no intention of meeting.

Madame Sainte-Beuve was asleep when he arrived and to his disappointment the housekeeper told him that Mademoiselle Riccardi had left half an hour previously. The housekeeper had been disapproving. Mademoiselle Riccardi was needed at Lancerre as nurse, and yet had scarce spent five minutes there today.

Maurice had flicked his whip infuriatedly

against his boot, knowing that his chance had been lost. He needed to take Marietta with no suspicious eyes watching. To have come across her alone at Lancerre would have been ideal. They could have been halfway to Evray before her presence was missed. He strode the ornately-decked room that so irritated Léon, wondering when next his chance would come, and his thoughts were interrupted by the sound of Marietta's hurried arrival.

With a satisfied smile he heard her run up the stairs towards his cousin's room. Slowly he walked to the foot of the stairs, preparing to mount, but he had no need to do so. She was already on her way out of the room, closing the door behind her, her cheeks flushed, her eyes unnaturally bright.

He waited for her, one foot on the bottom stair, one hand on the heavily carved banister. An elegant figure in fashionable dress.

'Oh!' Marietta gave a startled cry and then quickly recovered herself. It must be Elise's wedding guest from Montpellier. Seeing his intention of mounting the stairs, she said, 'I am afraid Madame Sainte-Beuve is asleep at the moment.'

He smiled. It was a strange smile and there was a curious light in his eyes. His face was abnormally pale, and as she drew nearer she saw that it was powdered. He made no effort to move out of her way.

'It was not my cousin I wished to see, Mademoiselle Riccardi. It was yourself.'

'She is recovered from the fever, but will need rest for many weeks,' Marietta said, unable to think of any other reason for his wishing to see her but concern for his relative's health.

'And so is not receiving visitors?'

'She is quite able to do so when awake,' Marietta said, pausing in front of him, wondering why he did not step aside and let her pass. His perfume was overpowering, sweet and cloying.

'But there is no one visiting at the moment?' His voice had a silky edge to it that was not at all pleasant.

'No.' She stepped forward resolutely, intent on making him give way for her. He moved his satin and silk-clad body further into the centre of the stairs.

'You seem in a hurry, Mademoiselle Riccardi. Perhaps I may accompany you a little way?'

'I'm quite used to riding unaccompanied.' She wanted to be away from him. She disliked his manner, his perfume, his smile, his eyes.

His gloved hand caressed the orb of the banister, the sunlight shining full on the giant-sized diamond, making it sparkle with a thousand fires. Marietta stared at it hypnotically. She had only ever seen one diamond of that size before, and that had been on the hand of the man who had visited her grandmother. The man who had then sought her out and had her burned. The man Léon had seen in the inn yard at Evray. The man who was now seeking her. The man sent by La Montespan to silence the Riccardis.

Slowly she raised her eyes from his ring to his face. Her fear was complete.

'No!' she cried, trying to push past him. He seized her arm, pinioning her hand behind her back.

'Your screams will only distress my kins-woman and serve you no good purpose,' he said viciously as he struggled to hold her.

'No!' She kicked vainly, twisting, biting. The smooth leather of a thong slipped over her wrists, jerked tight so that she cried out in pain.

'I think you *will* ride accompanied, Mademoiselle Riccardi,' he mocked as he forced her, still struggling, out into the courtyard. 'It will be a long ride, and your last.'

Marietta's cry for help died in her throat. There was only Elise and the housekeeper and the servants. Elise was too weak to rise from her bed, even if she heard her screams and there was nothing the servants could do. The wheel had turned full circle. She would die as fate had intended, on the pyre on Valais Hill. But not submissively. Never that.

She kicked out savagely and the powdered face flinched, the lines of dissipation and cruelty deepening. It was the face of a man no older than twenty-seven or twenty-eight, yet it was a face ages old. The hideous face of death.

'Cause me trouble and it will not only be yourself that dies, but the Lion of Languedoc also. He has harboured and protected you, knowing you for a witch; against that charge even he will be defenceless.'

As would Jeannette and Céleste, for once the de Villeneuve name had been tainted with witchcraft there would be no end to the persecution. She had wanted nothing but Léon's safety, and to gain it she would have to pay the highest price possible – that of going to her death in unprotesting docility.

She sat her mare, her back straight, her head held high.

'To Evray?' she asked impassively, as a goose-girl hurried her flock out of their path.

'I think that would be – most suitable,' he said, as if talking of an ell of cloth and not the place of her death.

She wondered if he was fulfilling his mission for La Montespan for favours in her bed or for money. Most probably for money.

She knew instinctively that her own body held no fascination for him, and was grateful for the fact. That sort of humiliation at least she would be spared. Maurice's lovers would be those of his own kind, if a man such as he was capable of love.

She wondered how he had endured charming Céleste. That must have been hardship indeed for him. And all to find out about herself! Poor Céleste, to be such a bad judge of character that she could not see beyond the slightest veneer. Lucky Céleste, for at least she was alive and would continue to be so for years and years, bearing children. Perhaps even children with the name of de Malbré.

She would not think of Léon, or of his feelings when he received Henri's message and found her gone. Of what his suffering would be. He would recover. He would marry Elise and she would be nothing but a memory to him. Marietta closed her eyes against the pain. She had determined not to think of him, but it was impossible. He filled her mind and her heart and she would go into eternity with his name on her lips. The knowledge of his love for her would give her the courage to endure the flames without crying out for mercy.

The road they were now riding she had not ridden since first approaching Chatonnay with Léon. Maurice had long since cut her bonds, sensing her capitulation. The sky was tinged with the first hint of dusk. It had been dusk when she had sat her horse so disconsolately, facing Trélier's inhospitable walls. Dusk when Léon had spurred Saracen back, saying ungraciously, 'You will be safer at Chatonnay than in Trélier'. They rested only long enough for a change of horses, and the next morning entered Toulouse, passing the inn where she had fled from Léon, cantering past the alleyway where he had caught her and kissed her.

The hours passed. Days merged into nights. There was another change of horse and yet another daybreak.

Surely that was the stream where they had sat and he had given her bread and cheese? She had not eaten for so long that she could no longer judge distances or for how long they had been travelling. Ahead of them the road was lined with plane trees, reminiscent of the drive leading to the château, and also of somewhere else. Marietta felt dizzy and sick. They had ridden down such a road, she and Léon, the morning after they had outwitted the Inquisitor. It had been hot and the trees had given welcome shade, as they did now.

Her heart somersaulted and her breath caught in her throat. Ahead of them were more trees, a sea of trees. And above them, piercing the skyline, Valais Hill.

All too soon they were deep in the forest and their track became familiar, and then, before she scarce had time to gather her wits, the trees thinned and Evray was before them. And people, running barefoot and excited, were shouting.

'The witch!' 'The nobleman has captured the witch!' 'The Riccardi wench is returned!'

They ran from every direction, clamouring around the pair on horseback as if in anticipation of a feast day.

'The witch is back!' 'There'll be a burning after all!' 'Go for the innkeeper!' 'Go for the Inquisitor!' 'Marietta Riccardi is returned to die!'

'And you let her go?' Léon's fury made even the Duke flinch.

'There was nothing I could do to stop her.'

'The Devil take you,' Léon said savagely, wheeling Saracen around and heading furiously back to the road.

Henri spurred his horse after him, calling out: 'Where are you going?'

'After her, of course, you fool! To Venice!'

'She may still be at Lancerre,' Henri shouted helpfully. 'She had Elise's dress with her.'

Never had the road to Lancerre been travelled so fast. Henri's horse, given full rein for the first time in years, skidded to a halt in Elise's courtyard, his nostrils flaring.

'I haven't seen anything,' the housekeeper was saying, clutching at the corners of her apron. 'Madame's cousin came from Montpellier, and now even he has gone, and without so much as a goodbye.'

Léon pounded up the stairs, wrenching open the door of Elise's room so that Elise screamed, drawing the bedclothes up around her throat. 'What is it? What has happened?'

The lace for the wedding gown lay across the bed.

'When did Marietta bring the gown?' Léon demanded harshly.

'I don't know, I was asleep. Oh, what has happened? Why are you looking like that?'

'Because Marietta has gone!'

Behind him Henri's voice called: 'Léon! Léon!' with such a note of urgency that Elise felt she would die of fright.

He ran into the room, the nonchalant, elegant Duke de Malbré; ran in like a village boy, clutching Léon's arm, saying, 'Cécile is here to see the housekeeper. She's full of the talk in Montpellier.' He paused for breath and Léon nearly shook him.

'What talk?'

'That Madame Sainte-Beuve's wedding guest is the man hunting down the She-Devil.' Léon's face whitened. 'Céleste met him earlier today. Cécile saw them together.'

'Earlier? What time?'

'Before Marietta left Chatonnay with the gown. Before he arrived here and made his presence known to the housekeeper.'

Their eyes held while Elise clutched at her pillows, crying hysterically, 'What has happened? What's the matter? Why is Léon so angry? Henri! Henri! Please tell me.'

He turned from Léon to comfort Elise and she clutched at him pathetically, sliding one arm up and around his neck, oblivious of the presence of her betrothed.

'Henri! I'm frightened! What is it? I'm so frightened! Please don't let Léon frighten me any longer. Don't leave me alone with him. I don't want ever to be alone with him again!'

'I promise you, Elise, I will never leave your side after today.'

'Never?' She clung to him.

'Never.'

Léon had no interest in them whatsoever. He was already running back down the stairs. As he did so Raphael entered, brushing the dust of the road off his sleeves. One look at his friend's face was enough to make him lose all his composure.

'What's the matter?'

'Marietta is being hunted as a witch,' Léon said tersely. 'She came back here with a gift for Elise, and now both of them have gone.'

'*Both* of them? I don't understand...'

Raphael was already swinging himself back up into the saddle, determined to be included in any excitement.

'The witch-hunter is your rival for Céleste's affections. Elise's cousin by marriage.'

Henri ran into the courtyard.

'Where the devil would he take her?' he asked. 'Montpellier? Toulouse?'

'No.' Léon sat his horse, curbing his impatience for action. He must think. Not Montpellier or Toulouse. No town where he, the Lion of Languedoc, would hear of it. Paris? No, for Marietta would voice her accusations against La Montespan. Then where? Where in God's name would he take her? Where would he have her tried and burned as a witch without causing any further speculation?

'Did you see anyone leave Madame Sainte-Beuve?' Henri was asking the dark-eyed goose-girl. Thin shoulders shrugged beneath a tattered dress.

'Only the lady who nursed Madame, and a nobleman like yourself. No one else. No one who shouldn't have been here.'

'Which way did they go?' Henri asked, motioning Léon to stay silent. One word from him and he would terrify the child out of her wits, and they would get no information whatsoever. The girl pointed obligingly and Léon and Henri rode off at full tilt. It was only Raphael who hesitated and asked, 'Did you overhear anything? What were they saying?'

He proffered a gold piece. The dark eyes shone greedily as she held her hand out for it. 'The lady asked if they were going to Evray.'

Raphael tossed her the coin, galloping after the receding figures of his father and Léon.

'Evray!' he shouted at the top of his voice. 'Marietta was asking if they were going to a place called Evray.'

Léon felt a leap of certainty within him. Evray! What a fool he'd been not to think of it himself.

'What about fresh horses, provisions?' the Duke asked.

'We'll buy fresh horses as we need them and we'll eat in the saddle. And we'll summon every able-bodied man between here and Toulouse to ride with us.'

'By the Mass, but this beats courting,' Raphael said, wiping his sweat-streaked face as he rode at Léon's side.

Léon did not reply. He had no breath for idle speech. He had thought by now to have overtaken the dandified Maurice with his protesting prisoner, but there had been no sign of them. It seemed as if they were riding as hard to Evray as they themselves were. And the minute they arrived the wood would be gathered for Marietta's funeral pyre – if it had not been done so already.

He whipped his horse the harder, desperate for a sight of Marietta's red-gold hair, but the road ahead was persistently empty and his fear increased minute by minute.

'More ale!' was the general cry as Marietta was dragged from her mare and nearly submerged by the jostling, hustling villagers.

The leather thong around her wrists tightened cruelly as Maurice pulled her after him, the gloating peasants making way for him as he strode towards the grassy track that led up the hill.

'What about the trial? The Inquisitor waits for her.'

'Then he'll have to wait,' Maurice answered grimly. He had no time for trials. The sooner his mission was accomplished and he was back on the road to Paris, the better. 'Is the fire ready?'

'Has been these last few weeks. No rain neither, so should be a grand blaze!'

Twice Marietta fell to the ground, only to be hauled painfully to her feet.

'What about the witch's mark?' the innkeeper shouted hopefully.

'No time,' was the rejoinder from his friends, and the innkeeper swallowed his disappointment and tried to forge a way to the front of the crowd, to be amongst those able to lay rough hands on Marietta as she was tugged and pulled higher and higher up the hill. She had reason to thank Maurice for his callous treatment of her on the journey; her long lack of food and water had rendered her almost senseless. The grinning faces around her seemed to swim and merge; the voices a cacophony of noise she could make no sense of.

The stake had been driven deep in the ground, the brushwood piled high around it. Her legs and feet were scratched and bleeding as, aided by willing hands, Maurice hauled her high on to the wood, slipping the free end of the thong around the stake. The sea of faces parted for a moment as the Inquisitor strode towards her, his black robes flapping in the evening breeze like a giant bird of prey. The sun was sinking fast, sucked down over the horizon in a blood-red haze.

'The witch's mark!' 'The witch's mark!' Leering faces taunted as torches were quickly lit and passed from hand to hand to enable everyone to see the spectacle. Maurice shook his head tersely at the Inquisitor.

'There's no time for anything but the burning.'

The Inquisitor asked no questions. He

knew from whom Maurice had been sent, or thought he did, for the forged letter of authority La Montespan had given him bore the seal of the King himself.

'What are you waiting for, fool? Set light to it,' Maurice shouted above the clamour, the nape of his neck prickling with that sixth sense that so rarely let him down. It did not now, but it had come too late. From above the noise of roistering peasants came another, far more terrible noise. The thundering sound of scores of hoofbeats.

The ground beneath them shook and the bewildered populace turned from Marietta, casting frightened eyes towards their village. They were too far into France to be raided by the Dutch or Spanish. What army was descending on them in such fury? The women screamed as the riders broke from the forest, pouring through the deserted streets of Evray, galloping up the hill, swords in hands, daggers held high.

Maurice took one look and grabbed the nearest torch, thrusting it deep into the wood. There was a crackle and a surge of flames. The crowd surrounding Marietta turned to flee from the oncoming avengers, and as the smoke from the base of the pyre rose around her Marietta could see Léon mowing down all who stood in his path, his face hardly recognisable as he laid about him with his sword, urging his horse through the seething mass of scattering humanity as he strived to reach her in time. She was coughing now, choking as the smoke thickened and the first flames flared deep in the heart of the brushwood, licking nearer and nearer to her bare feet and legs.

Maurice unsheathed his sword, cursing his lack of forethought in not bringing his horse up the hill with him. He lunged at Léon as Léon's horse broke free from the last of the villagers. Léon's terrified eyes were on Marietta, on the flames scorching her tattered gown, searing her feet.

The blow struck home, slicing deeply down Léon's arm, but he was scarcely aware of it. As Maurice regathered his strength for a more fatal thrust, Léon leapt from his horse, scrambling up the now flaming wood, heedless of the burns to his hands as he struggled to set Marietta free. His knife sliced through the leather thong and with maniacal strength he hurled her free of the flames, rolling her on to the bare ground as Raphael kept Maurice at bay.

The Duke had suppressed his disappointment at finding the Inquisitor unarmed, and made do with terrifying that gentleman to within an inch of his life, whilst the men who had ridden with them hounded the villagers down the hill.

One minute Léon's weight was on top of Marietta, rolling her over and over, his hands beating at the sparks in her hair and at the tongues of flame engulfing her gown; and then he was gone, flinging Raphael aside and crossing swords with Maurice.

They circled the blazing pyre, cutting and thrusting, Léon's injured arm hampering him, the blood running freely. Raphael leapt forward as Léon lost his footing and Maurice's sword flashed downwards, but he was not needed. With a kick of his boot Léon sent his adversary tumbling backwards, Maurice's high-heeled boots skidding on the grass, his arms flailing wide in a vain attempt to regain his balance as he fell backwards into the heart of the flames.

Léon and Raphael rushed forward, grappling with his boots as they struggled to reach him and pull him free. The blazing heat drove them backwards and Marietta hid her face in her hands, unable to watch as the hungry fire devoured her enemy.

'Come, sweet love. It's time to go home.'

Tenderly he drew her to her feet, wincing with pain as he did so.

'Your hands,' she whispered. 'You've burned your hands.'

'And will a few more scars make such a difference to your love for me?' he asked, dark eyes gleaming.

'Nothing could make a difference to my love for you,' she said, gazing up into the face that she had thought never to see again.

'And yet you told Henri you were leaving me.'

'Only because of Elise. Because of what I heard the Abbé say.'

'And so you would ruin Elise's happiness, as well as mine and Henri's, all for a few overheard words?'

'I wanted to preserve Elise's happiness.'

'Then let her marry Henri, for she desires nothing else.' His voice thickened. 'And I desire nothing else but you, Marietta Riccardi.'

He bent his head and kissed her and then, eternities later, Raphael said, 'I have a horse for Marietta.'

'She doesn't need one,' Léon answered. 'We'll leave Evray as we did before, only this time will be the last.'

'And the Inquisitor?' Marietta asked as she mounted Léon's horse behind him. 'What of the Inquisitor?'

'You need have no further fears of him,' Henri said grimly. 'He thought you a genuine witch sought by the King himself, an idea I have disabused him of.'

'And all those men? I thought it was Louis' army, the way they charged up the hill.'

'They are in a way, for they are some of the men I can always call upon to fight for

284

me in the King's cause.'

'Where are they now?'

'Doing what soldiers always do. Enjoying themselves.'

From the village came the distant sound of carousing and female laughter. Gently he spurred his horse into movement, and Henri and Raphael followed them down the hillside and once more into the forest where he had first found her. The moon rode high and the sky was thick with stars, the night air warm and heavy with the scent of wild rosemary and jasmine. Her arms were around his waist, her head against the reassuring broadness of his back.

'I shall have to start another lace gown when I return to Chatonnay,' she said dreamily.

In the darkness Léon smiled. 'You'll have no time for such fripperies. I intend to marry you immediately, even if it means you wearing nothing but your shift for the ceremony!'

She giggled, her arms tightening around him. 'That wouldn't please her at all! She wants a gown of *point de Venise* lace. A *full length* gown of *point de Venise* lace.'

'Who does, sweet love?' he asked in an amused voice as fireflies danced a farandole in the darkness around them.

'Oh, just someone,' Marietta said, her lips curving in a secret smile as she thought of their merry-faced granddaughter with the dimples in her cheeks. 'Someone who would be most indignant at having only a shift for a wedding gown.' And she closed her eyes in contentment as they cantered steadily southwards.

The publishers hope that this book has given you enjoyable reading. Large Print Books are especially designed to be as easy to see and hold as possible. If you wish a complete list of our books please ask at your local library or write directly to:

Dales Large Print Books
Magna House, Long Preston,
Skipton, North Yorkshire.
BD23 4ND

This Large Print Book for the partially sighted, who cannot read normal print, is published under the auspices of

THE ULVERSCROFT FOUNDATION